"A Collection of Words from the Roundtable" is an eclectic mixture of intimate and personal experiences and remembrances—not only of the Jersey Shore, but of life in general. Kudos to the ten writers for a job well done.

Don Stine, journalist and owner of Antic Hay Books, Asbury Park NJ

"A Collection of Words from the Roundtable" is filled with eclectic stories and interesting voices from this Bradley Beach writing group.

Patricia Florio, author of "My Two Mothers," Ocean Grove NJ

Reading "A Collection of Words from the Roundtable" was such an enjoyable experience for me, one that I'd like to share with anyone who loves fine writing. The stories and poems are the creations of ten talented local writers, among them several septua-, octa-, and nonagenarians. Certainly there is much nostalgia, both of the humorous and heartbreak variety. The stories, essays, poems, and tributes evoke the special human bond of familial love and friendship enduring over several generations. Through their unique experiences, the authors were able to convey this love of family and friends and elicit from this reader many smiles, chuckles, and even tears. After reading all the literary gems and being able to distinguish the various styles, I felt that I had known these genuinely talented writers and had shared their experiences with them as longtime friends.

I will proudly keep a copy of "A Collection of Words from the Roundtable" at the library of the Stephen Crane House in Asbury Park. Stephen, his mother and his sister, all local Jersey Shore writers of the late 19th century, would surely approve.

Frank D'Alessandro, Stephen Crane House, Asbury Park NJ

A Collection of Words
from the
Roundtable

A Collection of Words from the Roundtable

The Harriet May Savitz
Writers of the Roundtable

iUniverse, Inc.
Bloomington

A Collection of Words from the Roundtable

iUniverse books may be ordered through booksellers or by contacting:

iUniverse
1663 Liberty Drive
Bloomington, IN 47403
www.iuniverse.com
1-800-Authors (1-800-288-4677)

ISBN: 978-1-4759-4168-5 (sc)
ISBN: 978-1-4759-4169-2 (ebk)

Printed in the United States of America

iUniverse rev. date: 01/22/2013

Table of Contents

Dedication

The Writers of the Roundtable of Bradley Beach dedicate this work in memory of our beloved founder, mentor, teacher, friend and author.

May 19, 1933 – July 20, 2008

HARRIET MAY SAVITZ

We continue to write in her memory and want to share the gift of words she has taught us. As we sit at the Roundtable, her knowledge, encouragement, and inspiration remain part of our writing. She taught us to believe in ourselves and to use words to let others explore what we have experienced during the past century. The written word is magical. Whether the pages are filled with words of truth or fiction, they give the reader the escape into knowledge, history, mystery, adventure and love.

Harriet May Savitz has written over thirty books in her lifetime. Her children's books, essays and knowledge of how to improve the lives of those with physical disabilities are a legacy that will live forever. Harriet may no longer sit at our Roundtable, but her spirit still guides us.

Special Acknowledgments

This book would not have been possible if it weren't for the hard work and dedication of the following people:

James P. Gorman—who developed the concept and layout of the book and photographed the back cover.

Irene Maran—who designed the front cover.

Milton Edelman—a professional photographer who is responsible for the black and white pictures for the authors' biographies.

Gary S. Crawford—who was instrumental in the editing, finalization, and publishing of the book.

Introduction

The Harriet May Savitz Writers of the Roundtable is a writing group comprised of over a dozen people who attend a weekly hour-and-a-half writing session. We encourage our members to bring an original piece of work—a poem, story, or written paragraph—of something they have recently composed. Each individual reads his or her work and the others offer helpful critiques.

Most of us are published writers and authors, our work appearing in newspapers, magazines, or books. Our purpose for publishing this book—*A Collection of Words from the Roundtable*—is to emphasize our group's individual work and talent and to highlight each specific writing style. We wish to expand our fan base beyond our members by reaching out to the public and inviting them into our literary world. Our stories represent themes about people from all walks of life.

We hope you enjoy the selections of work exhibited in our book and we encourage you to share your favorite stories with others. There is no greater joy for a writer than to have a complete stranger compliment his or her writing skill.

Irene Maran, Director
Harriet May Savitz Writers of the Roundtable
Bradley Beach NJ, January 6, 2012

"Words don't die. Words don't grow old.
Words go beyond the page they are written on.
Time returns through the written word."
—Anonymous

Now

Let's Meet Our Authors . . .

Ruth J. Abramowitz, Gary S. Crawford, Milton Edelman,
James P. Gorman, Irene Maran, George H. Moffett,
Elia R. Monticello-Reyes, Alice Cooper Richardson,
Kalinka Shumanov, Rebecca Wasson.

Author's Biography

Ruth J. Abramowitz

Ruth Abramowitz lives in Asbury Park and is a published writer and author. She started writing poetry and essays at age twelve. Her writings record a history of the past, present, and foretell a hope for the future. *From Horse and Buggy to the Moon*, her first book of essays, was published in December 2007. She firmly believes that life is a gift we share with others. She spent her career years as an executive secretary employed by government agencies and private industry. Her motto is, "Live one day at a time."

Email: ruthja90@hotmail.com

Synopsis Of Writings

Story #1 . . . The Farm
  Family life on a farm during the 1920s.

Story #2 . . . Remembering Mom
  Lessons learned and memories of childhood days.

Story #3 . . . Ninety Years Plus
  Years don't really matter
  It's the way you make them count
  It's the love that you put into them
  And the joy that you take out.

Story #4 . . . 2010 Christmas Blizzard
  How weather and environment change our lives.

Author's Biography

Gary S. Crawford

Gary S. Crawford is a published author and local historian. He has published two books and many print and website articles on area historical subjects, as well as a horror fantasy novel. He is considered an authority on the Morro Castle ship disaster. Long active with many local non-profits, he has handled publicity and public relations for these groups. Raised in Neptune City, he lives in Neptune with his wife, grown daughter, and three grandchildren. He has been a member of the Roundtable since March 2011.

Email Gary at: gary@GarySCrawford.com
Online: http://garyscrawford.com

Synopsis Of Writings

Story #1 . . . Release the Angels
>A lesson in the proper way to respect and enjoy distilled spirits.

Story #2 . . . Tough Old Bird
>A coming-of-age story of a girl who had everything go wrong for her, only to rise up from her despair to triumph.

Story #3 . . . We Call Them Bennies
>A look at visitors to the Shore Area and how they got their interesting nickname.

Story #4 . . . Third Grade Remembered Looking back at the ways things used to be, or at least as we remember them.

Author's Biography

Milton Edelman

Milton Edelman is an 89 year old World War II veteran who resides in Bradley Beach. He is a renowned professional black & white photographer. His collection of photography of Asbury Park in the 1950's shows currently in the Gallery in Asbury Park. His hobbies include writing, photography, and a vast knowledge of submarines. He is best known for his one line humorous observations known as "Miltonisms."

Email Milton at: vintagephotosbymiltonedelman@gmail.com

Synopsis Of Writings

Story #1 . . . Ode to a Candle
> A poem based on the symbol of a candle:
> Will the flame stay lit, long enough for romance to bloom, or
> will it lose its glow?

Story #2 . . . The First Marriage
> The author uses satire to reveal something that was missing in
> The Bible; a comical approach that made Eve an honest woman
> and saved mankind from being born out of wedlock.

Story #3 . . . Close Call
> The author, a World War II veteran, looks back at a moment
> in time, with his finger on the trigger, and makes a split
> second decision that would have changed the lives of two men
> forever.

Story #4 . . . Two Poems
> The author turns inward, safe in his mother's arms, and then
> outward, to the sea.

Author's Biography

James P. Gorman

James Gorman is a 63 year old, recently retired, disabled Vietnam Veteran. Employed by the U.S. Government as a Computer Analyst for 25 years, he's lived with his lovely wife, Doreen, in Bradley Beach for 15 years.

Hobbies: writing, movies, any of the arts and anything and everything Irish.

Favorite book: "Catcher in the Rye" by J.D. Salinger

Favorite music: Lyrics by singer/songwriter/Rhodes Scholar Kris Kristofferson

Favorite quote: "Some people see things as they are and say why. I dream of things that never were and say why not."—George Bernard Shaw

Email Jim at: exlkhrst@yahoo.com

Synopsis Of Writings

Story #1 . . . Memories of a High Tide
> The tides of the ocean cause a young man to look back and reflect on his early childhood. He remembers the close relationship he had with his grandfather when life was simple and the world exciting.

Story #2 . . . The Message
> The author goes on a literary quest searching for answers to philosophical questions that may hold answers to life's mysteries.
> He finds the answer to the biggest challenge of mankind.

Story #3 . . . The Reader
> The author pays a sentimental tribute to his deceased father, who opened doors and pointed his son in the right direction.

Story #4 . . . The Famous Holiday Fire of 1997
> A family pet creates mayhem and a picturesque and tranquil snow-covered scene becomes a tragic event to remember on a chilly Christmas Eve night.

Author's Biography

Irene Maran

Irene Maran is a retired high school administrator who resides at the Jersey Shore. She enjoys writing children's stories and humorous essays about life. Irene currently writes a bi-weekly newspaper column for *The News-Record* of Maplewood/South Orange and *The Coaster* in Asbury Park. She loves all aspects of nature and takes great pride in nurturing her grandchildren, cats and turtles, and reading her stories to the students at Bradley Beach Elementary School and local libraries. Her hobbies include painting, illustrating her books, making beaded bookmarks and creating original jewelry.

Email Irene at: maran.irene@gmail.com

Synopsis Of Writings

Story #1 . . . Anger Management
> The everyday life in a thrift shop full of unusual and eclectic characters.

Story #2 . . . Golf Ball Island
> Three young children, under a grandmother's guidance, explore and claim Golf Ball Island for their very own.

Story #3 . . . Hats Off To Lilly, a Budding Writer!
> The youngest child in the library reading group proves to have the greatest potential in becoming a writer.

Story #4 . . . The Lunch Box List
> How I intend to complete my lifetime list of doables.

Author's Biography

George H. Moffett

George H. Moffett is in his early eighties, having spent his first seventy years living in the Borough of Bradley Beach enjoying the many beachfront activities Mother Nature provided. Those summer escapades were why *Chicken Soup for the Beach Lovers Soul* published his essay "One More Wave." The essay was also chosen by a local book club as the best essay in the *Beach Lovers Soul* book. Twice George's writings have been published in the *Chicken Soup for the Recovering Soul Daily Inspirations* book. His writings have also been printed in newspapers including the *Asbury Park Press* and *The Coaster*.

George attended Bradley Beach Grammar School, Asbury Park High School and Monmouth University. He has been a surfer, a U. S. Marine, a banker, a municipal Borough Clerk/Treasurer, a municipal Council member, and an active Methodist church member; all of which have been resources for his writings. He likes to write about feelings—his own and those of others—including crying which he admits to doing. George writes from his heart about life's experiences.

Email George at: geomoffett@yahoo.com

Synopsis Of Stories

Story #1 . . . Crying
    This writing traces the value of crying in one's life by turning it
    from a negative into a positive. In so doing maybe others will
    see the value in their own tears.

Story #2 . . . One More Wave
    To me, Mother Nature's beach was everything good whether
    you were seventeen or in your seventies, and whether it was
    summer or winter. The life of escapism on the sandy beaches
    presented adventures from building sand castles and playing
    running bases to dozing off on the beach with the warm sand
    contoured around your body and your mind full of the fantasies
    of summer. In the winter months, quiet and serene walks still
    stimulated the mind.

Story #3 . . . The Silent Bell
    This chronicle traces the ringing of the church's bell to remind
    the community of the activities of their church. The bell became
    silent for many years until one individual couldn't tolerate the
    silence any longer. A movement was started, and with the help
    of the youth of the church, the bell started ringing again.

Story #4 . . . My Summer Book Reading Escapades
    Some of the many intricacies of reading are revealed in this
    writing, starting with my teen years when I read for enjoyment
    and entertainment, right up to my early eighties when I now
    read for enlightenment and growth. Reading can open so many
    new doors for you to walk through.

Author's Biography

Elia R. Monticello-Reyes

Elia R. Monticello-Reyes was born and raised in Newark, New Jersey. She graduated from Barringer High School and received a certificate from the Small Business Administration upon completion of an extensive business course.

She married Joseph M. Reyes in 1947 and had three sons. Elia worked as an executive secretary and treasurer for her husband's business, A & R Cabinets & Millwork, Inc., which he owned and operated.

In 1975 she accepted a position with the Superior Court of New Jersey in the Special Civil Parts Division and retired as a Principle Clerk.

She moved from Maplewood and now resides in Bradley Beach. Elia is a long—standing member of the Harriet May Savitz Writers of the Roundtable.

Email Elia at: eliagreg1@juno.com

Synopsis Of Writings

Story #1 . . . Christmas in the Depression
Simple joy and merriment of the holidays during the Depression.

Story #2 . . . My Father Nicola
The adventures of a young teenager who traveled from Silvi, Italy, to America.

Story #3 . . . A Tribute to My Brother Nick
A sister's pride and memories of her younger brother who meant so much to their family.

Story #4 . . . My Girlfriend Corrine
A lifetime of cherished friendship remembered.

Author's Biography

Alice Cooper Richardson

Alice was a private practice counselor for many years in Portland, Oregon. She counseled couples and her specialty was working with psychiatric aspects of physical illness. She led a physician's support group for two years and then took a position in a locked psychiatric hospital as a Mental Health Therapist for thirteen years.

Alice began writing when she was eight years old in order to express herself and for the pure joy of creating. She has written intermittently all her life. She now writes light humor and interesting life stories.

Email Alice at: aliecoop@netzero.net

Synopsis Of Writings

Story #1 . . . Capsized
> The adventures of a group of adolescents on the Hudson River.

Story #2 . . . The Resurrection
> A tale of one woman's problems with an errant hearing aid.

Story #3 . . . Two Teachers
> A story of role reversal.

Author's Biography

Kalinka Shumanov

She was born in Sofia, Bulgaria, but her family moved to Belgrade, Yugoslavia, where she grew up. Kalinka's family experienced the horror of German occupation and the terror of Communism. She chose to study medicine, hoping to help the world, but finally her family decided to escape from Communist Yugoslavia. They landed in Italy, and after 3 years of being "displaced" persons, arrived in America. They finally enjoyed the freedom and world opportunities. Her children were born here and escaped the unstable world she had left. Kalinka worked as a microbiologist for 25 years and after retirement, worked as a substitute teacher and court interpreter. Now in her seventies, she enjoys reading, writing and painting. "I think I deserve it."

Email Kalinka at: dnazdrave1@verizon.net

Synopsis Of Writings

Story # 1 . . . The Unforgettable Easter of 1941.
    The day that changed my life and taught me the evils of war.

Story # 2 . . . My First Thanksgiving in America
    I learned about an important holiday in America and some people's kindness.

Story # 3 . . . The Person Who Most Influenced My Life
    My grandmother, who taught me humanity and inspired me to enter the medical field and work for human health.

Story # 4 . . . Our Cat Pookie
    The antics of an adopted member of the family.

Author's Biography

Rebecca Wasson

Rebecca Wasson lives in Summit and Bradley Beach with her husband. She completed her undergraduate degree at the University of Hawaii and her Masters Degree in Education at Kean University. Rebecca is certified to teach school in California, Hawaii, and New Jersey. She loves spending time at the Jersey Shore with her family, especially her only grandson, of her only daughter. Her favorite saying is by Anais Nin: "We write to taste life twice."

Email Rebecca at: <u>wassonrebecca@ymail.com</u>

Synopsis Of Writings

Story #1 . . . Camaraderie on a Summer's Eve
   Friends enjoying music and friendship.

Story #2 . . . Summer Shine
   Analysis of a single mother whose children are her flowers.

Story #3 . . . Tales from the Left Coast
   The author chronicles her love of Santa Barbara, California,
   where she resided with her late husband

Story #4 . . . Our Town
   The author laments about occurrences in her town that are
   upsetting, but then comes to a realization.

The Farm

Ruth J. Abramowitz

My father brought his family to America from Russia in 1912. Many families from Russia, whom they knew, lived in the Brownsville section of Brooklyn. His parents and nine siblings decided to live there. Dad remained in New Jersey where he was living with my mother's family, after arriving in America in 1909 at age sixteen. He met my mother when she was fourteen and they married six years later in 1915. Dad's dream was to own a farm and raise his children in the Catskill Mountains. In 1919, for $180.00, he purchased 140 acres of land with a ten room farmhouse and a barn. The house had no plumbing and was heated with potbelly wood stoves. Electric lines were being installed and would take six months to complete. Lighting was by kerosene lamps attached to the walls. My father was five foot seven inches in height. A strong body, dark hair and brown eyes, Dad loved the farm. At 4:00 in the morning he was in the barn milking the cows, feeding the horses, and gathering eggs from a dozen chickens. By 5:30 he was in the kitchen putting milk into containers to store in the icebox and eggs into a box coated with hay so they wouldn't break. Then he went outside to the well and brought water into the house for cooking and washing. This was a daily routine, and his dream was coming true.

Mom was a city girl and did not enjoy being a farmer's wife. She hid her disappointments because she loved my father and wanted him to be happy. With two small children, ages four and two, and no modern facilities, it was hard caring for them. I was born in 1920, and plumbing was installed that summer. It was easier for mom with a bathroom and running water in the sinks. I remember there was a long pull string from a tank full of water above the toilet that we pulled to flush.

In the summer our house became known as a rooming house. My aunts and their children would come to spend their vacations. Families came and rented rooms for a couple of weeks or the entire summer.

They brought bed linens and utensils for cooking with them. Shelves were given to each family and ice-box space for perishable food. Dad took orders and delivered what each woman wanted from the town store. Sometimes a couple women would go with him. The country store was a large wooden building that sold clothing, shoes, toys, groceries, farm tools, and medicine. You could also look in the Sears catalogue and order. At the back of the store behind a window was the postmistress. She handed out mail and sent out our letters.

The roomers were families recommended by friends and relatives from the city. They lived in the same communities and their children went to school together. Vacationing on the farm meant they could continue their friendships without being separated during the summer months.

The kitchen had two stoves, two sinks and a large working table in the middle of the room. The women had a time schedule when to use the kitchen. Bath time was in the evening before bedtime. One or two women worked in the kitchen with Mom. This kept the heat down and gave those working more space. Tables in the dining room were assigned to each family. Some days we would have picnic lunch on the lawn, or eat on the porch. Cold food was served during breakfast and lunch. Two days a week, Mom would prepare scrambled eggs for the children's breakfast.

I remember the rocking chairs and small tables on the porch where we played when it rained. I liked the summer because there were children to play with. Mom was smart and knew how to make the women feel each was special. The children loved her. When problems came up, they went to her for advice. She never took sides and would tell everyone, "When you live under one roof, you become a family. We need to respect and care for each other." I felt these families were part of mine. They returned year after year to be with us.

I didn't like winter. It was cold with many snowstorms. In 1923 during a blizzard my brother was born. He was delivered by a midwife, who lived down the road. She came with her two sons in a horse and wagon. The baby came out looking blue and was dipped into hot water, then cold, to make him breathe. Mrs. Budd was praised for saving his life and our families became close friends. The Budd boys often came to help Dad with the livestock. A rope line from the house to the barn was strung, so Dad could find his way through the deep snow to the barn and care for the animals.

In 1925, everything changed. Mom was told she needed major surgery and we left the farm. My father's youngest brother came to care for the animals and house. A few months later, while he was in the barn, the house caught fire and burned to the ground. We never learned what started the fire, and no longer had a farmhouse to live in. With no money to rebuild, my father decided we should stay in the city. He gave the farm to my grandparents to use for their vacations. Members of the family built bungalows and the farm became a summer retreat.

My family remained in the city and Dad's dream of farm life was ended.

Release The Angels

Gary S. Crawford

'Tis surely a shame to hear of someone overdoing his intake of fine Irish or Scots spirits. With the love and labor poured into each drop of these fine whiskeys, the souls of these very men who, many centuries before, had perfected their respective waters of life—*Uisce Beatha*—Celtic liquid gold—that made their very names well known even today, would be turning 'round in their graves should they hear of the misuse and abuse of their fine spirits.

Although many a man believes he has perfected the art of bending his own elbow, a bad night followed by a bad morning after 'tis sad proof that he has indeed failed.

One does not hurry perfection, you see. Time and effort goes into the distilling of fine spirits, and a man who takes all that time and talent invested and simply gulps down the product, well sir, certainly does not deserve the very privilege of tasting such quality fare! Worse still, is the man who gulps down the whiskey, and then has the audacity to chase it down with a glass of water! A terrible waste, I tell you! If you can't handle the taste, sir, then remove yourself at once from this public house! The very idea—chasing away the taste of perfection.

You see, some tender loving care—and responsibility—of your own are in order here, to fully appreciate the quality in that glass before you. That golden liquid has gone through such complicated tasks to become what you see before you; including the malting, the roasting, the distilling, the careful mixing and blending, and most important, the aging, to bring you what you see here today. You must give proper respect to your beverage.

As the whiskey ages in charred oak barrels, a portion is lost to evaporation. Those in the know call this "the angels share". So expect to lose somewhere around three percent of the volume in that barrel, even more if aged beyond twelve years.

So in that time, the tiny angels become immersed in the liquid in those barrels. So tiny, they are, that it takes them a full twelve years to consume just that small amount of whiskey. They don't take much, so no one minds, and it surely never hurts to have a few angels on your side, now does it?

And when the whiskey is properly finished, and poured from the oak barrels into the individual bottles to be sold, the tipsy angels, not quite understanding all of the sudden jostling, also wind up in the bottles. This they don't quite care for, as those barrels were nice and dark inside, and now there's light shining into the bottles. Well, sir, this can make them a wee bit cranky.

So now, that bottle of whiskey, with its tiny population of tiny cranky angels, has arrived to your local pub, and you've ordered a drink from it. Out of the bottle and into your glass they come, still a wee bit tipsy, and still a wee bit cranky.

So now you've got a choice to make: release the angels from your glass, or swallow them and face the consequences later.

Quite simple, really. A veteran of the whiskey wars, as it were, knows to allow the glass of spirits to breathe for a few moments, to settle after the sudden turbulence of being poured, and to allow those important ingredients to mingle once again. And to allow the angels to calm down a bit.

A knowing man will order a glass of water alongside; not to chase the whiskey, but to provide the means to release those angels. Just a few drops of water, often just sprinkled from the fingertips across the top of the whiskey, will allow those miniature creatures to climb from the glass, dry their tiny wings, and fly back to heaven. You can see them if you look close, but they are so easy to miss. Bid them hail and farewell; merry we meet, merry we part, and merry we'll meet once again.

For your part, you have saved yourself from the wrath of those tiny beings by not swallowing them. No sir, you'll not be wanting to do that! Why, they get angry and through the night they'll rattle 'round inside of your head and belly, they will! They want out. They don't mind being trapped for however long in the whiskey, but inside of you? Believe me, they'll show you who's in charge.

And next morning, as you nurse your sore head and upset belly, you'll be wondering how all this came to be.

Very simple, my friend. Next time, just remember to release the angels.

Ode To A Candle

Milton Edelman

You took the match so eagerly
And burst quickly into flame
You listened ever so quietly
As we dined and chatted away

You graced our dining table
You cast a warming glow
The beauty of your flickering
You really loved to show

At times you flickered knowingly
When we wanted another to know
And never, never a sound from you
As your flame moved to and fro

Now that we have dined with zest
Glowing within and without
But, as happens with all good candles
I now must put you out

Memories of A High Tide

James Gorman

I recently went to the beach on one of those blistering August days when the sun is so bright and the air is hot and a bright blue cloudless sky beckons you to the ocean. I jumped into the dark blue surf and immersed myself in the pounding waves of its cool temperature. I dove through waves as the salty brine was absorbed within all my pores, coming up drenched and surrounded by white foam. After a while I came out invigorated and refreshed. I sat myself down as the sun's rays pierced through damp salt air. Taking a clean white terrycloth towel, I patted my face and from that towel and salt air I remembered summers long gone by.

I remembered sunny days when bright rented colored beach umbrellas dotted white sandy beaches. Noxzema was the only way to protect from the rays of the sun. The beach was a pirate's sand and the treasure was the largest seashell that could be found. The waves were bigger then or so they seemed to be. I also remember walking through backyard gardens until I came to the rear of Grandma's rented house. The water still played an important part, for taking showers in the outside wooden stall was a must before one could enter. As bathing suits hung out on the line to dry, the smell of Grandma's cooking permeated the air. There were other smells of whiskey and beer that later I would come to know and respect. It was a not really a house but a big Victorian mansion with one room in which we resided.

After a fine dinner just as the sun was to set, the cool night air would start to approach. We would go out on the old wooden front porch where friendly strangers would creak back and forth in old wooden rocking chairs. I was introduced to each and every one by my proud grandfather.

They would pat my head and say kind things, though none of them I can now recall. I would ask if we could go on the rides. Can we go on the rides? Can we go on the rides? Can we pretty please go on the rides,

I would persistently say? And then off I would go with my over-loving, over-caring kind grandfather. He would take my hand and with his straw hat, sweet smelling pipe and beaming pride intact, we would go off into the dark night air to an enchanted land where innocent imagination becomes reality. I can recall those lights and sounds so clearly now. Do you want to go on the whip first, then the bumper cars and save the roller coaster for last or how about the haunted house, penny arcade and then the Ferris wheel? Oh what a delightful choice I was given. I could smell the popcorn as we passed by the man that was always trying to guess your height and weight. The whip would spin me around on every turn as all faces turned into a laughing blur. The rhythmic sound of the carousel could be heard as we ate a hot slice of pizza and washed it down with a syrupy sweet Coke, all for a quarter. He lifted me up on the counter as I rapidly fired the air rifle at the passing ducks. Then we tossed coins on the red & green tile dots or was it plastic rings around wooden bottles? Sometimes I can't recall but knowing him, it was probably both games we played. A stuffed animal prize was always won but not for victory, just for trying. It turned out that Grandpa had connections.

My hands were sticky from half-eaten cotton candy as I tied balloon strings on my arm. We rode the big wooden roller coaster at the end of the night. Up and down the steep hills and valleys of the steel tracks we soared into the night with speeds and sounds that overshadowed our white knuckle screams and fears. The night ended on the boardwalk, where lemon ice or a soft vanilla ice cream cone was dripping down the back of my hand as the sky burst forth with Wednesday night fireworks. Glaring rockets of all shapes and sizes pierced the blackness above our heads as showers of brilliantly colored lights dazzled us down below and I so loved the bright white light and loud explosions that no matter how many times you said it wouldn't, it would still make you jump and twitch.

So many August summers have gone by since then, way too numerous to count. Three years ago I drove back on a sentimental journey and saw that time had taken its toll. Both the roller coaster and Ferris wheel are gone. In fact, my childhood memory was covered over with a black asphalt parking lot with a convenience store. A question that comes up whose answer might only be of interest to myself and maybe Holden Caufield is when there are no more carousels, where do hand painted horses go? Perhaps they are caked with childhood dust in an amusement retirement farm. It is no longer economically feasible to have fireworks light up the night's sky and sweet syrupy Cokes have been replaced with a pre-mixed carbonated formula. I passed by the old Victorian house that still stands and there are old people with nameless faces that still creak back and forth on rocking chairs. Both my grandparents have been dead for many years, good kind people that they were. May their souls rest in peace.

When I think of it, time is so cruel, it took everything. It took away dear loved ones, painted horses and glowing skies, youthful innocence and a grandfather's pride. But alas! The answer is that I am able to think of it and time is not that cruel at all because it left behind white terry cloth towels, salt water, sea breezes and ocean waves that will never go away. And these are all I need to trigger and jog my memory so over and over I can relive my happy youth.

Anger Management

Irene Maran

I volunteer at a local thrift shop once a week. The few hours I spend tagging and selling useful and unusual items is always refreshing and self-satisfying. We accept clothing, kitchen appliances, glassware, toys, garden items, etc. There's always a variety of people from all walks of life shopping or browsing, many of them repeat customers. We have serious shoppers looking for a great bargain, curious shoppers who are just window shopping, never purchasing anything, and those who stop by to break up their day by socializing.

Mrs. Kravitz, is a regular visitor on a mission. A slightly built senior with grey hair and round wire glasses, she is an avid collector of vintage umbrellas. On one of her visits to the shop, Mrs. Kravitz luckily stumbled upon three very old Victorian umbrellas. She returns regularly hoping to find more, but so far has been unsuccessful. This eccentric woman sashays in weekly wearing a long skirt, her hair twisted in a bun and neatly tucked under a big stylish hat. Her trademark is a pastel colored parasol which she carries in winter and summer, rain or shine, looking much like an old fashion post card.

Another weekly customer, Mrs. Silver, consistently comes in dressed to the nines. She carefully examines every article of clothing in her size, always searching for designer label clothes. She wears them well, although they were never purchased in a department store, but in our thrift shop. We have nicknamed her the "Designer Label Lady."

The "Cap Man" drops by looking for caps of all types and sizes. Baseball caps with team logos line the back of his car window and are his good luck charms. "No bobble head dolls for me or my car," he exclaims, "Just caps, the more tattered the better and dirt cheap at that."

A favorite customer of ours is Tom. He comes in every few months and heads directly for the kitchen and appliance section. Tom never needs assistance because he knows exactly what he wants. Marching in carrying a large wire crate, he fills it to the brim with dishes. He's not particular about the size, design or color. Counting the plates as he stacks, Tom just keeps piling them in. Some people stack pancakes, but Tom stacks dishes. One day while checking out at the cash register, Tom's bill came to $20.00, high for a thrift store where some items start at five cents. When I asked him what he intended to do with all these dishes ranging from twenty-five to fifty cents, Tom said "I run an anger management class where my members throw them against a wall. It's a good way to let out aggression and release tension." I was told by a fellow worker that Tom had been fortunate enough to find a pair of boxing gloves in the store which he snapped up quickly. It was probably utilized as another technique in his anger management program.

When Tom left, I wondered if there were figures painted on the wall with recognizable faces at which members hurled their plates. I would think that a direct target of some kind would produce quicker results. I'd like to sign up for Tom's class just to relieve some of my own aggression occasionally. After all, I believe that this fast moving world of today makes us all grind our teeth and want to break something every now and then.

Crying

George H. Moffett

"Here I go again" are the words that indicate tears are on the way. It happens when I am talking about something so near and dear to my heart. Like helping a youth from a broken home, being given a genuine heartfelt "thank you" from someone I was able to help through a crisis, or memorializing a dear friend who passed away. I get really upset when this happens as it interferes with the orderly flow of my thoughts as I fight to remain in control and express myself. Am I embarrassed when this happens? No, not now. However, in years past I would forgo expressing a deep-seated emotional thought to avoid the pain and embarrassment of losing control, of crying.

I recall a few years ago when a dear life-long friend, a business associate, and a public servant passed on and I was asked to speak at his church funeral service. There was so much to say that I had great difficulty condensing all my thoughts. At 2:00 a.m. one morning, I woke up out of a sound sleep, started writing, and in two hours my "Celebration of Life" eulogy was complete.

Now I was faced with the real challenge: how to deliver the eulogy in a manner that my composure, or lack of it, would not in any way detract from the message. To accomplish this, I didn't sing any of the hymns, listen to the scripture reading or listen to what the pastor was saying. I stayed out of the main sanctuary until it was my time to speak. When my appointed time arrived, all went well until I started my very sentimental conclusion and "here I go again" took over. I cried. It was devastating to me but not so to the mourners which I learned afterward.

The mourners were gracious with their comments and I felt they were being sincere. To them, it was a positive experience as they felt my pain, but they also felt the depth of my love for my deceased friend and understood my anguish.

I realized the words had to be spoken and I had no regrets for speaking them. Maybe my tears were positive and helped the mourners to realize that we all lost a great person and a great friend.

Now I cry from strength and courage, not from weakness and fright. Now I express my deep thoughts. I am more self-confident; I am a secure person. I must have realized the futility of years of giving in to negative habits, which always produced negative results. How did this growth come about? Like all growth, it came about through change. You change a bad habit by replacing it with a good habit. It was so simple. Once I changed, I became amazed at how simple it was to change and then I really became so annoyed and frustrated with myself for having wasted so many years of not growing, of not changing.

Does crying embarrass me? It did, but not anymore. I am now confident enough to reveal my honest emotions and feelings. I realize it is more important to share them with others in the hope that they will see the value in doing so and maybe, just maybe, they will see the value in their own tears.

Christmas in the Depression

Elia R. Monticello-Reyes

Many years ago, when I was a little girl, I remember that our landlady would give my family the Sunday newspaper which included the comics.

The Christmas holidays were approaching, and my sister Dolly and I wanted to decorate the house. We decided to cut up the comics of the Sunday newspaper into little strips. A paste was made with flour and water. The strips were joined together with the paste and made into long chains. We hung them around the kitchen for a festive holiday look.

The black coal stove's glowing flames were keeping us warm. Mama baked cookies and Papa made cordial drinks into pastel colors. The holiday cookies were arranged decoratively onto platters while the colorful pastel cordials were poured into fancy bottles.

Family and friends exchanged their specialties with each other as the sounds of Christmas carols played on the wind up Victrola, with Mama and Papa singing along.

My sister Dolly and I went to bed wondering what Santa would bring us.

Christmas morning, Mama came into our room to tell us that Santa had arrived with our gifts. To our delight we each received a beautiful doll. Santa knew what we had wished for.

Capsized

Alice Cooper Richardson

When I was twelve, my brother became a sea scout. They learned about seamanship, more knot tying than the boy scouts and they learned about sailing.

When I was twelve I loved the idea of the sea scouts. I wanted to be a sea scout. No girls allowed. I also had a crush on one of my brother's best friends in the scouts. If I recall correctly, his name was John Ridout.

In my first writing of this, I wrote, "John was hot!" But we didn't use that phrase back then. We had no names or expressions for the young men who made our hearts go pitty pat.

On the Fourth of July weekend, the sea scouts were taking their sailboat out. Somehow I got invited along, to my everlasting joy. And against all the rules.

It started as a quiet day on the river. We sailed into the middle of the Hudson. I was loving every minute of it, watching John handle the boat. Enjoying the air, the sky, the water, the river and mostly John.

A very large motorboat roared past us, creating a giant wake and we capsized. I came up under the sail realizing I would have to dive to get out from under (and afraid of losing my glasses on this ill-gotten voyage) only to see my brother diving under the sail to find me.

We hung on the sides of the boat; the scouts discussing what to do. Their first priority was getting rid of me since I wasn't supposed to be there. It was decided that since John was the strongest swimmer, he would swim me the half mile to shore.

Now as I have heard in years since, one of the stupidest things one can do after an accident is to leave the boat. I didn't know that then and I was so enchanted with John I agreed to make the swim.

The first thing John said to me was "Ditch the shoes." The second that he said was "We'll swim slowly and we'll make it." We started off, my shoes on the bottom of the Hudson River, swimming at a fairly leisurely pace. Always moving slowly towards shore.

Out of nowhere boats began appearing, circling us. We were hauled out of the water and wrapped in blankets. We could see many other boats circling the overturned sailboat and taking care of my brother, the other scouts and the boat.

The river had been so quiet. Where had all these boats come from?

The man, who had hauled John and me out of the river, said to us "You kids are so lucky!! You are soooo lucky!!! The engineer on a train going by saw you capsize and began tooting S-O-S on the train's whistle. Every boat within hearing distance has been searching for whatever that train was alerting us to find."

And that is how I came to be rescued from the Hudson River by a train.

The Unforgettable Easter of 1941

Kalinka Shumanov

There are moments in life we never forget and it changes our future and the way we look at the world. Such a moment was April 6, 1941, for me and millions of other people that were witnesses or victims of the unexpected, unprovoked, monstrous attack of Hitler's army on Serbia, part of the former Yugoslavia.

Easter in Eastern Europe is a very religious, respected and enjoyed holiday. The weather is usually beautiful, winter is over and nature is awakening with colors, aromas and hopes for a summer of fun. The whole country was waiting for the beginning of spring and a new year.

I was dressed in my new colorful dress and decorated hat, eager to go to church and meet my friends and show off my new outfit with pride.

It is impossible to describe the horror that interrupted this lovely time. Bombs began falling from the sky, houses crashing down like children's toys, deafening noises, dust and objects flying all over. My father, a soldier from WWI, ran out to see what was happening and soon returned covered with dust and his face was very red and burned. "Belgrade is on fire, God help us." We were occupied by Hitler. Our life was changed instantly and for a long time, 5 years. There was no food, water, electricity, heat or any medicine when we needed it most. Due to lack of normal hygiene and no drugs, many infectious diseases developed.

People of today can't imagine being without most essential daily needs; water, food, heat, sanitation and contact with the rest of the world for a long time. Many people died but survivors were never the same. I suddenly grew up from a happy healthy teenager into a fearful and nervous adult; I was only 13 years old.

The only good thing after this horrible change of normal life for all the people in beautiful, prosperous Serbia was that the people became close to each other and helped one another.

Farmers started to bring food to the city. For a long time they were unable to come, with roads being destroyed and afraid of being robbed or killed. It took 5 years to rebuild the city.

Every year for Easter my memories are resurrected and I am thankful to heroes who brought the peace back. Again humanity prevailed.

Camaraderie on A Summer's Eve

Rebecca Wasson

Oftentimes the best made plans for an outing with friends are most enjoyable when there is no advance planning made at all. An impulsive decision to do something different can be fun. Would you like to join us for a concert Saturday night at the gazebo in Bradley Beach? Let us escape the oppressive heat in our homes and go oceanside to be enchanted by the smooth voice of Keith Franklin resonating in the summer breeze.

So we picked up our friends at their houses along with walkers and bags of goodies. Keith enchanted us with the reincarnated voices of Frank Sinatra and Dean Martin. We sang along and swayed to the sounds of the music while enjoying each other's company. Soon a group of four people became a group of six, when a husband and wife strolling along the boardwalk saw us and joined in. The group of six became a group of eight and then nine when we saw two more people and another from our senior citizens club. At final count there were about ten of us at the gazebo.

Former friends, new friends, boardwalk strollers and Saturday night concert regulars were all joined together. We enjoyed being serenaded by the familiar music sung by a talented musician, accompanied by the salty air, the neon moon, and the summer breeze, but most of all by the camaraderie.

Remembering Mom

Ruth J. Abramowitz

One day I came home from school and heard my sister say "Mom's home." Those were the best words I remember hearing during my teenage years. Mom had several operations during those years and we were told she might not come home from this one. Running into her bedroom and seeing her sitting by the window was a wonderful sight. She looked pale and had lost a lot of weight, but her face had that same wonderful complexion and smile as she opened her arms and I ran into them for a hug.

As a child I remember Mom sitting in front of the mirror brushing her long golden hair, which flowed down her back below her waist. She was a heavyset woman with a very large bosom. That bosom was my comfort zone when things went wrong and I needed to feel safe. She had deep blue eyes and an inviting smile.

Watching as she braided the long tresses of hair, twisting and turning them into a bun was fascinating. I kept wondering how she could do that and still finish in time to feed and clothe five children waiting for breakfast. Mom never came downstairs in a nightgown or housecoat. She was always dressed in a simple dress, stockings and shoes. She wore an apron to cook and clean and when Dad came home was looking fresh and pretty.

My mother was a smart woman, way ahead of her time when it came to dating boys. She would tell us to double date the first time and bring the boys to meet her and Dad before going out. Her advice was that it's more important to be respected than to have a lot of dates. If someone isn't a nice person, you can avoid him or her, and if you can't say something nice about them, keep quiet.

She taught me about being charitable. I was two years old when she took my hand and put two pennies into it and said, "Put them into the charity box." A small blue wooden box stood on a shelf above the stove. Every Friday night, Dad gave each child a penny or two and we would put them into the box. As I got older I remember complaining I wanted to keep the pennies for ice cream or candy and Mom would explain that other children needed clothing and food and the pennies would help them. She never refused anyone who came to our house for help and my friends loved her. They came to ask her advice instead of their own parents. She would tell them not to be afraid to speak with their parents. Another lesson I learned was as long as we told the truth, the punishment was not too hard to take.

I was in my late thirties when I became a mother and soon learned motherhood is not easy. I also learned the love of a child is priceless. Mom lived into her eighties and I had her in my life for over sixty years. I am now in my nineties and it has been many years since I saw her face or heard her voice. The lessons she taught and the memories I have can never be forgotten or replaced. There are many days I recall those wonderful memories and know she is still in my life.

Tough Old Bird

Gary S. Crawford

She was born a tough old bird. The last of four kids, she could hardly be called The Baby. Right from the start she had to work her way into the hierarchy of her siblings. She was walking—and running—before she was a year old. She skipped "toddling" altogether. She had enough words in her vocabulary by then to make herself understood. And she could hold her own when it came to gaining the attention of a parent or two.

While just a pee-wee, she was the neighborhood tomboy. Even though she was little, she was never picked last for a team. She was forever sporting an orange mercurichrome-painted knee or a Band-Aid or two. And when she came home with a black eye or a fat lip, you were assured the other party was in worse shape. Once her dad had to pick her up at the police station after a skirmish with some older boy. The boy's parents were horrified that their dear sweet son had gotten a licking, but when they saw the little girl responsible for it, they decided that pressing charges would be most embarrassing. While her mother was fit to be tied that her little girl had been arrested, her father bought his Little Outlaw ice cream on the way home. Her mom just said that she marched to the beat of a different drummer.

And then puberty crashed down upon her. The wiry little tomboy suddenly became tall and ungainly. Her body started to develop and was all out of proportion with itself. She was all legs, with two very clumsy left feet supporting them. Her face became—in her own words—a cross between a pizza and a red relief map of the moon. Her hair became an oil refinery, requiring at least two washings a day. Her mother cut her hair short to help with the grease problem, but the bowl cut hairdo did little for her self-esteem. Her eyesight began to suffer and she was now forced to wear ugly new glasses for her new nearsightedness.

Those who had once been her friends now talked behind her back, and the nicest nickname they used for her was Big Bird. Boys who used to like her would now avoid her like she had the plague, while making her the butt of terrible jokes and rumors.

She cried herself to sleep almost nightly, wondering who was doing this cruel thing to her and why.

But during the summer between junior and senior years, she grew into herself. Her complexion cleared, revealing fine smooth skin. Her eyes adjusted and she could see again without those terrible glasses. Her hair was now soft and shiny and long. Her body caught up with itself and now she could be described as a "masonry outhouse".

On the first day back to school, many wanted to know who the new girl was. Guys who teased her unmercifully now had the nerve to ask her out. Her old friends, the Beautiful People who had shunned her, wanted to be friends again. She rejected them all, and remained friends with the clique of bottom dwellers and geeks she had found herself among during those skank years.

She'd had enough of high school and after graduation, took a few months off before joining the US Army. There was no college money left in the family treasury so she joined the military to take advantage of the GI Bill and the scholarship money available.

She found herself stationed in Saudi Arabia during Desert Storm, and in a military hospital after a SCUD missile was intercepted above her camp, causing much damage on the ground below. With a broken arm and shoulder, she got a little time off and came home, with her Purple Heart, and all her old "friends" from school wanted to come visit her, the new hometown hero. You can just imagine what she told those people, and it wasn't, "Gee, I'm so glad to see you!" She resisted attending her twenty year high school reunion, but gave in and went with some of her old geek friends. She did enjoy herself, once she saw that the once-pretty popular girls were now round and soft and fertile, and the handsome jocks were all now fat and bald and funny-looking. There was justice, after all!

Still a thoroughly independent free spirit, and still quite a looker, she owns her own business, owns her own home, and doesn't need a husband to make her complete.

You just gotta love your little sister.

The First Wedding

Milton Edelman

Adam and Eve never got married. Therefore, they were living in sin. Yet . . . amazingly, these two people were responsible for the begetting of an entire planet of billions of people. Unfortunately, it sends the wrong message to many of today's young couples who simply choose to live together rather than join in holy matrimony. The institution of marriage is necessary for the orderly upbringing of offspring in a civilized society.

Therefore, as a pre-qualified fiction minister, I will perform the holy vows for the first wedding, indeed the first wedding ever performed on Earth, for Adam and Eve. This event will be minus snakes or apples, to provide the moral link to the current generation. Though I may be guilty of plagiarism, in addition to Adam and Eve, I will create an angel called U-Mo-Du to perform the ritual necessary to ordain the sacred union of the first humans to ever to set foot on this earth.

It must be understood that as a novelist I have the power to be Godlike; literally, to create people, places, times, directions, and do with them as I please Whereupon U-Mo-Du spoke to the first two naked shivering beings, saying, "Until I complete this unprecedented ceremony, both of you will remain ten paces apart, and Adam, no touching until I return." And so U-Mo-Du searched far and wide and produced an olive branch. Then U-Mo-Du proceeded by saying, "Come together and both of you will hold hands on opposite ends of this branch. At my command you will break this branch in two and you will both become as one." And so it happened. U-Mo-Du solemnly declared them husband and wife and told them to kiss. "But wait until I disappear, and then you may begin to beget in total privacy. And since no one is looking, except for the two doves in yonder tree, you may remove the fig leaves without fear of shame."

Hear ye, hear ye, without the signing of any papers, without throwing of rice, without elaborate gowns, tuxedos, catered affairs, limousines, flowers, or "just married" signs, I married Adam and Eve.

From this day forward and forever more, clergy everywhere will have the credible evidence to preach the institution of marriage to all mankind.

Though I may boast of performing the greatest act on Earth, I have but one regret: I forgot my camera.

The Message

James Gorman

Most avid readers have a certain genre they prefer to read, such as romance or mystery novels, both fiction and non-fiction. I myself have always wanted to learn something while reading so I chose books that covered the wide spectrum of religion, psychology, philosophy and New Age.

I read excerpts of the Bible, works by Wayne Dyer, Deepak Chopra, Plato, Saint Thomas Aquinas, teachings of Buddhism, Confucius and the Dali Lama. I was looking for a common thread that, once understood, would provide the key to unlock life's mysteries. I discovered a profound book, "The Celestine Prophecy" by James Redfield. It was very important that it did not go against my Christian beliefs.

The idea is that there are no coincidences. People, be it family, acquaintances or total strangers, come into your life for a reason to leave you a message. These messages are extremely subtle and are filed away in our subconscious mind. A day, week, or even a year may pass before we recall these messages and react in some way. We may receive 30 or 50 messages a day depending upon how many people we come in contact with. Besides receiving messages, we also relay messages, based on our mannerism and experiences. In order to comprehend the messages as they are received, we have to slow down and have a heightened sense of awareness and focus. It would be like fine tuning a radio station to remove all static and receive perfect clarity. Messages we provide or accept can either be positive or negative. It depends on how we eventually process the information.

Ten years ago there was a visiting priest during the mission at my local parish. His sermon would change my way of thinking and how I viewed the world.

He spoke of the greatest message of all is the "Spiritual Message" that comes from our Creator, the message of "Love, compassion and forgiveness". The love and compassion are easy to comprehend but forgiveness is the most important and the biggest challenge. If we refuse to forgive, then the pain and hurt stays within our heart, mind, and soul. Forgiving and healing go hand in hand—you cannot have one without the other. [If you can remember one fact from this story, the act of Forgiving is entirely different than Forgetting]. Two different words—forgive and forget—almost spelled the same with two separate and distinct definitions. As shocking and as difficult as this may sound, we should forgive the Japanese for Pearl Harbor, Hitler for the Holocaust, and yes, even bin Laden for Sept. 11. History is inevitable no matter what the outcome. If nations do not learn from their mistakes, they will be repeated. Eventually we will all be judged; but it is not for us to judge.

Recall the greatest man who ever walked on earth and the greatest tragedy that ever happened: The Crucifixion. When our Savior was dying on the cross, He looked up to the heavens and said, "Father, forgive them, for they know not what they do". He never said, "Forget them, Father, this never happened."

There have been billions of people before us and there will be billions after we are gone. Individually we have on an average 90 + years to get it right. My readings and studying over the years has brought me to the belief that our whole purpose on earth is for mankind to learn how to co-exist.

Now that you have read, heard, and been given "The Message", it is your decision to agree or disagree. Every person on the planet is a microscopic element of both the problem and the solution. My purpose is to give you something to think about. The decision is totally yours. Be kind, compassionate, and positive in your words. To quote a song, "Let there be peace on earth and let it begin with me".

Golf Ball Island

Irene Maran

My son, daughter-in-law, their two children, and a friend came for a long 4th of July visit to the shore house. There are so many things at my home in which to entertain a child or adult that the name "Grandma's Resort" became its official title. My "resort" offers bicycles, skate boards, backyard swings, a hammock, horseshoes, a canoe and pedal boat. Since the house backs up to a lake, fishing is encouraged as long as everyone abides by the rule of "catch and release." Turtles and fish swim freely in this protected area.

There is a public golf course directly across the lake. Our pedal boat brings the children up close and personal to a small island a short distance from the golf course. This area is dotted with golf balls. My grandchildren have discovered this "pot of gold" nesting place for errant balls which have settled here as the result of a golfer's bad drive. They pedal out with nets and pails to collect stray golf balls imprinted with interesting logos. In addition to the Titleist, Top Flite, Hogan, Pinnacle and others, they have found a prize Yankee ball and a Looney Tunes character golf ball named the Tasmanian Devil.

"We're going to pedal to the island, stake our flag and claim the island," the kids chanted. Thinking of Tom Sawyer's adventures as a young boy, I gave the children an old tee shirt and magic markers to make a flag. When they were finished, it was attached to a long stick already adorned with an American flag. Being eco-friendly, they colored their flag green and printed their names and date on it. Three excited children with smiling faces climbed into the boat waving their flag as they pedaled to the island.

Mom, Dad, and a nervous Grandma rode in the canoe behind hoping to take pictures of this momentous occasion. You would think they had landed on the moon as they docked the boat, jumped out and unfurled their flag, hammering it into the sandy ground. "One small step for children and one giant step for mankind," the trio shouted as they named their newly claimed territory "Golf Ball Island." I felt like an explorer myself as an adrenalin rush surged through my body as I exited the canoe and stepped onto the sandy soil. I was happy for the children and hoped we weren't intruding on this small island in the middle of the lake at the edge of the golf course. The explorer part of me won out over the intruder part when I witnessed the flag being planted.

I took multiple pictures from every possible angle. Golfers from the fairway waved at us, probably wishing they could be part of this spontaneous, gratifying adventure. I'm sure they weren't aware of the fact that we were also scooping up all the stray golf balls that had veered off course. Feeling exhilarated to have shared in this experience with my grandchildren, I took a deep breath, and for a moment experienced the excitement of what it was like to be a child again.

One More Wave

George H. Moffett

I wasn't thrown out of the house as a kid, but during the lazy days of summer you wouldn't find me at home. I lived on the beach. Nothing could have been better. The beach was everything good: freedom from the chores of daily existence; warm gentle breezes; waves to ride back to the beach; sand to play games in; and seclusion, in the midst of a crowd, that promoted freedom of the mind, body, and spirit.

The beaches were much smaller when I was a kid, so they were more crowded than today. That didn't matter. We still played running bases with a tennis ball and tried to tag the runner out before he reached base. Errant throws usually ended up on a sunbather's blanket, sometimes hitting the person, but that wasn't my problem. I had to retrieve the ball, and in my haste to do so, I would deposit unwanted sand on their blanket and further annoy the sun worshipper. If I got the base runner out, it was worth the verbal abuse. If the sunbather came after us we hightailed it down to the water, jumped in, and had a catch skimming the ball along the surface of the water.

We also built intricate sand castles along the water's edge with protective walls to keep the water away from our castle. As the tide came in, we built bigger protective walls, but we always lost the battle. Mother Nature won once again. We just moved on to another game.

The beach also provided us with a free sauna. It was the sun-warmed sand to flop on and heat up a body made cold by the ocean. In the process it changed those wrinkled fingers back to normal and shed the body of all the goose bumps collected from an hour of energized horseplay in the ocean. It turned blue lips pink again, a signal that it was time to leave the warmth of the sand, run to my ocean and dive in. Experience guided us so that we reached the right speed, chose our perfect wave, and dove over it with the grace and composure of a carefree dolphin.

Finally, it was a chance for me to attack my buddies in the water, without making it obvious, by going beneath the surface and pulling them under and then swimming away. The best game of all was the piggy back fights in waist-high water with as many kids as were willing to risk it. We would attack the enemy and dethrone the opponent from the shoulders of his carrier. The last team standing was the tired victor.

Fun, but dangerous, was skimming. One would throw a round, thin board along the surface of extremely shallow water as it reached the beach. Jumping on the board we would try to maintain our standing position as we skimmed along the surface of the water. If you lost your balance or if the front edge of the board dug into the sand you would be sent flying totally out of control. It was worth the challenge and the danger.

But riding the waves was my favorite fun thing to do. Today boards are used, but when I was a youngster you used your body as the board. We perfected the art of selecting the "perfect wave" and riding it for several hundred feet, right up onto the dry beach. We mastered the ability to change directions at the last split second. To this day I can still remember the panicked look on the bathers' faces as we just skimmed by them, much to our enjoyment and much to their fright. It was the high of the day to end up on the dry beach. I would lay there savoring my victory for a few moments before getting up and charging into the water again to conquer another wave. It was always just "one more wave" that got me in trouble as I rushed home—wet, barefooted, and full of sand—trying to beat Mom's five o'clock deadline for supper.

As with everything in life, there was a downside to living on the summer beach. Sunburns, blowing sand, other bratty kids kicking sand on you, and the dangers of rip tides carrying you out to sea or waves slamming you into the ocean bottom were a few. But the worst intrusion was people invading the serenity of my existence as I dozed off while lying on the beach with the warm sand contoured around my body and my mind full of the fantasies of my own summer beach.

To me, the beach is everything good, whether you are seventeen or in your seventies, as I am now. In my later years I find that it still draws me into its world of escapism. I no longer spend time on the beach in the summer because of the strong sun and the crowds, but I do visit my old hideaway in the other seasons.

Now it is fall and the transition begins. The summer visitors from northern New Jersey have returned to their winter homes away from the shore while the parking meters and the lifeguard benches have retreated to their winter storage locations. The boardwalk concessions are still holding their ground, but they are boarded up for the long winter hiatus. Nature is taking control again.

My solitary, quiet, and uneventful walks along the edge of the water, protected with warm clothing to buffer me from the cold winds and the distant sun, still stimulate my body and my mind. They are a respite from the busy world of details and demands. When I walk on my beach now, I am enveloped in an aura of peace and serenity. My spirit, my soul, is strangely warmed in spite of nature's cold temperatures. I know life is still worth living. The simple things of life always bring me back to this realization: Life is good. My beach of decades ago, with all its activities of youth and excitement, beautifully meshes with my beach of today, with my deeper appreciation of its quietness and reassurance. As I walk along examining and picking up the fascinating shells by the water line, I am reminded that now is all I have. Now is all I need.

My Father Nicola

Elia R. Monticello-Reyes

My father, Nicola Monticello, was born on November 19, 1895 in Silvi, Provence Teramo, Italy, which is located on the east coast of the Adriatic Sea, a suburb of Rome. It is known as the Italian Riviera.

He was the youngest of three; a brother named Antonio and a sister Rita. At the age of seven he became an orphan and was raised by his brother and sister.

Nicola had an opportunity to come to America when he was a young teenager. A distant relative would be his sponsor. He sailed from Naples, Italy, on a ship named "Madonna." There were 1,364 passengers on the boat. Fifty-four were first class and 1,310 were third class. The ship was a "steam triple expansion engine twin screw."

Nicola Monticello arrived in New York on April 23, 1913. His name appears on the wall at Ellis Island in New York harbor.

He settled in an Italian neighborhood. His sponsor informed the owner of a nearby grocery store that he would not be responsible for any purchases Nicola would be making. He was completely on his own in a new world and struggling with a new language unknown to him. He boarded with Italian families and worked on construction jobs.

World War I broke out on February 24, 1918. Nicola enlisted in the U.S. Army. His basic training took place at Fort Dix in New Jersey. He completed his basic training and also received his American citizenship papers. He was very proud to be an American citizen. He was placed in the Combat Engineer's Unit and shipped to France on July 9, 1918.

In the Army he met two Italian comrades. They were to become lifelong friends and were godparents for each other's children. Their names were Joseph DeGiovanni and Ernesto Voya.

The war was ending and soldiers were submitting furloughs. My father requested to go to Italy to visit his brother and sister. He was told that it was unlikely it would be approved. He would continue to wait as all the others were returning from their furloughs. Months passed when finally his furlough was granted. He traveled to Silvi, Italy, to visit his family. He wore his American Army uniform and looked very handsome.

His sister Rita introduced him to a beautiful young girl. Her name was Filomena Selvaggi, my mother. He courted her during his furlough. When it was time for him to leave, he told her that he loved her and would return to marry her. They wrote romantic letters to each other for four years. As time went by, their feelings for each other grew more intense.

Filomena's family owned property with many olive vineyards, still owned by family members to this day. Her family kept telling her that Nicola was not going to return to marry her. Filomena still kept sending letters to him. One day she received a letter from Nicola asking her to come to America and they would be married. Filomena answered that letter saying, "If you want to marry me, you must come to Silvi for me." With that response, Nicola immediately made plans to return to Italy. They were married on April 6, 1923 in a small Catholic church, St. Rocco. They returned to America as husband and wife.

In her new world, Filomena had to adjust to unfamiliar surroundings and missed her beautiful countryside around the Adriatic Sea. She also missed the family that she would never see again.

Nicola and Filomena had five children; three sons, Michael, Nicholas, Rocco and two daughters, Elia and Dorothy.

Nicola Monticello received the Victory Medal and the Bronze Victory Button for his service in the Armed Forces in France.

The Resurrection

Alice Cooper Richardson

My hearing aid has had many lives. It strays from the path often and when discovered, claims like a born again Christian, "I once was lost, but now I'm found."

Not long ago I fell asleep on the sofa and when I awoke the hearing aid was gone. I had a suspicion as to where it had gone, but no idea why it had made such a journey. I was sure it was under the sofa. However, my sofa is built low to the floor. My hearing aid is too big to roll. To be under the sofa, it would have had to crawl.

I could not check it out. In front of my sofa is a marble coffee table I cannot move. Just as the hearing aid is too big to roll, the coffee table is too heavy to lift. Fortunately, after a couple of weeks a friend appeared. The table was moved. The sofa opened and Voila! The errant hearing aid, alive, well, no longer in hiding.

I swept it up with joy, offering it good wishes. Popped in a new battery to return it to full consciousness. We were back in business.

In late July as the temperatures soared into the one hundreds and sweat appeared like ticks on a hound dog, the hearing aid went out. It has an allergy to moisture and when any moisture hits simply says "Not tonight, dear, I'm feeling damp."

At that point I took it out saying "well, so much for you" and set it on the table before me. We were living—me, my dog, and my hearing aid—in our back room. The only room with an air conditioner.

The table was littered with my cigarette rolling supplies, a glass of ice water, an ash tray and some debris from fruit I had eaten. As the heat continued, the debris followed the Biblical injunction to "go forth and multiply" and multiply it did.

The heat broke last night. I returned to my bed with relief. The leather sofa in the back room, even with the air conditioner, had clasped heat to me as if I were shivering on the coldest night in Siberia.

This morning I got up. I looked at the mess. I took away the sheet that had not protected me from the sofa's hot embrace. I gathered up the dishes and the papers and the paper towels that I had been too hot to move. All whispered "shame on you, shame on you for leaving us here" as I deposited them in the trash.

I got dressed to go out and went to get my hearing aid from where I had left it on the table. No hearing aid. I didn't have time to pause, but as I left I could hear it calling me—from the trash can.

I did what I needed to go out and do and came home. It was heating up again. I got a glass of ice water and sat quietly for a while.

I could still the hearing aid calling me. "Yoo hoo—come and get me."

About two p.m. I got out a clean garbage bag, sat down and began working my way through the flotsam and jetsam of our trip through the temperatures of Hell.

Just as it had crawled under the sofa several months before, my hearing aid had managed to take itself to the very depths of that garbage bag.

I pulled it out, a bedraggled soul of a hearing aid. I brushed it off. I cleaned it. I dried it.

When it was safely in my ear it cooed softly, "Aaaaaaaah! Resurrected once again. I am reborn."

Music up—"Amazing Grace."

My First Thanksgiving in America

Kalinka Shumanov

Coming from Eastern Europe where we didn't have the tradition of the Thanksgiving holiday, with all the beautiful customs around this special time, I was totally unprepared. Since I did not speak English, I did not understand the significance of this historic holiday.

I became intrigued by the colorful decorations and advertisements in the wonderful autumn colors in my neighborhood, The Bronx, N.Y. where I lived. I called a woman I had met who was from my native Bulgaria, and asked her what the reason for all the excitement was. She gave me a brief history of the reason for establishing Thanksgiving 388 years ago. I was fascinated and felt that as a new immigrant, I should celebrate this historic event. Even though I had limited means, I decided to go shopping and buy and cook the traditional foods for this Thanksgiving Day. There was a little problem but it did not stop me from my determination. I was a new mother with a three month old daughter, Jasmine. My husband and I had very little money and of course, no car. I had a new baby carriage which was used for shopping and visiting different places. I put Jasmine in the carriage and went to the nearest food store, about one mile away. My baby was sound asleep by the time I got to the store. I had to move her to a much less comfortable shopping cart which I learned was the common practice when food shopping. I soon learned all the traditional foods for the holiday. When I started checking the different size turkeys and wondering which one I could afford, just then, the manager, an older man, tapped me on the shoulder and handed me a large turkey. With a big smile, repeating many times, "present, present, present, Happy Thanksgiving". I did not know what to do, I tried to smile and not cry as I was overwhelmed by his human kindness. This gentleman also helped me pack all the food in my baby carriage and again wished me "A Happy Thanksgiving".

My trip back home was not easy. I had to carry my daughter in my arms and negotiate the carriage full of groceries back to my apartment house. Unfortunately, there was no elevator in my building and I had to carry all the groceries up three flights of stairs all the time carrying Jasmine in my arms as my husband was working. After all the difficulties, I managed, and we had a wonderful feast on my first Thanksgiving Day in America and I will always remember it.

Summer Shine

Rebecca Wasson

When the chilly winter has completed its punishing course and school is finally over for the year, my family moves to our beach house in Bradley to enjoy the easier times in our lives. In the next town of Ocean Grove lives a very good friend of mine. Her name is Summer Shine. She has a family of four, two girls and one boy. Her son and my grandson call themselves brothers, brothers from another mother. They attend Bradley Beach Summer Camp together, having done so since pre-school. After camp they can be found playing video games, skateboarding, or engaging in some type of athletic activity. They never seem to tire of each other no matter how much time they spend together.

Summer works very hard, sometimes for many long hours. The men in her life have not lived up to their potential, so she raises her children alone. Her year old daughter Chloe is always smiling and happy. Her teenage daughter Raven is her responsible assistant. Everyone is well adjusted and happy. Summer's children are her flowers. On Monday morning she had to be in a meeting in Connecticut and my once-bachelor husband, who never had children, found himself with four of them. I told him not to worry, that all would be well and God would be kind to him if he helped. We quickly split the children into two groups. The boys went off to camp in one car with my husband, while Raven and Chloe drove off with me to day care in the other. As we all know, it takes a village to raise a child. I am the children's adopted grandmother; they call me Morning.

In her spare time Summer has created her own organic Chap Stick and Bath Salts, respectively called Summer Stick and Summer Salts. She was the first one to put feathers in our hair. Every year we have an argument because I am either spoiling or not taking good enough care of her children. Every year we make up. My dream for her is that someday one of her creative ideas amasses a fortune and she and her family live happily ever after. To wax poetic, come rain or shine, Summer Shine will always be a friend of mine.

Ninety Years Plus

Ruth J. Abramowitz

The pin read "90 and fabulous." The tote filled with presents said "This is one incredible 90-year-old." My sister, who lives in Florida, hosted my party at her daughter's home in Connecticut. Many relatives were invited but, due to weather and travel conditions, could not attend. It was a small gathering but a lot of excitement and enjoyment. Stewart, my godchild, and Beverly, his wife, drove from Ohio to spend this special time with me. Louis, my nephew, who I last saw twenty years ago, took a train from Rochester, New York. Looking into the smiling faces gathered to greet me was the most wonderful gift anyone could give me.

I've seen and learned much during these years. There is still a lot to learn and I ask our Creator to give me years to complete a second book and contribute what I can to make this world a better place. I have experienced everything from birth, education, love, motherhood, tragedy and death. I watched the wonderful science and technical breakthroughs that sent us into space. Our communication system connects us in seconds to places and people throughout the world. Hand held cyber phones give us immediate access to information and individuals. We are technically connected, but in my mind we have lost the human touch. With all the wonderful advancements in our lives; technology has brought problems that deprive us of privacy and help the evil minded find ways to disrupt and destroy.

Looking back, I continue to compare my teenage days to those of today. We left our doors open so anyone could visit at any time. We met in friends' homes, playgrounds, parks, and favorite eating places. I feel nothing replaces the touch of a hug, and speaking face to face gives a better understanding to our words.

The winter of 2010 proved the coldest on record with storms, earthquakes, floods, tornados and hurricanes destroying complete communities. The world as we know it is disappearing. All our advanced technology can't stop Mother Nature from showing her powers are stronger than any technical machinery made by human hands.

This July, I will be entering my ninety-first year. The next generation will find themselves in a new world. History books (if we still write books) will tell stories of what used to be.

My experiences of love, friendship, joy, sorrow and knowledge have given me a blessed life. If I were asked would I change my life? My answer would be "No". The hard times made me stronger to face the challenges that are part of being alive. I look forward to future birthdays.

We Call Them Bennies

Gary S. Crawford

Every Memorial Day, a strange mass exodus of vehicles falls off the Parkway and heads due east. Within these vehicles are a curious lot, a species of human being we call the Benny.

We see them everywhere; blocking the roads, filling up the restaurants, burning themselves on the beach. And leaving their money with us.

Most of we native Clamdiggers can point out a Benny easily enough, but how did they get that curious name we call them?

Years ago, before widespread use of automobiles and good roads, visitors to the Shore got here by train. And they brought luggage. Lots of it. Since railroad coaches couldn't hold much in the way of carry-on luggage, most of the larger items were carried in the baggage car. And like luggage carried on airlines today, the pieces had to be tagged to state origin and destination.

The Central Railroad of New Jersey hauled roughly half of the visitors to the Shore, with the Pennsylvania RR bringing the other half. CRRofNJ handled a lot of travelers to and from New York City and North Jersey and the luggage was tagged to reflect this. Cardboard tags read BNENY, for Bayonne, Newark, Elizabeth, and New York. Baggage handlers nicknamed these items "Benny Luggage" and the name stuck. Soon the owners of the luggage were also called Bennies.

It should be noted that the railroads were experts at handling baggage and few if any pieces went astray, unlike your favorite airline of today sending your luggage to Denver when you are flying to Florida.

And as a side note, most of the cast of the TV show "Jersey Shore" would also qualify as Bennies, one of the nicer names we have for them.

A Close Call

Milton Edelman

As a private during WW2, I was assigned to a temporary job as a clerk in the base guardhouse. My duty was to type out the morning report of all of the men incarcerated each day, and other guardhouse chores. At times I would make announcements through the door which had bars on the top half. One prisoner would come over to the door and make taunting remarks to me which I ignored, thinking he was some kind of whacko. Normally, the military police would escort prisoners to the mess hall, the infirmary, or other places.

One day, for some reason, the sergeant told me to take an inmate outside to police the grounds, which meant having the inmate take a coffee can and pick up butts, candy wrappers, matchsticks, and other trash.

So I strapped on a Colt .45, which I had fired at the firing range during basic training. It was literally a hand held cannon. I brought out the prisoner, who just happened to be the one who seemed like he was looking for trouble. For a while he picked things up while I stood guard at a safe distance. The he started to come to me slowly. At a certain distance which I deemed too close, I told him to stop. He kept coming slowly and I said "Halt". Still he kept coming closer and again I said "Halt", and I pulled my weapon. He made another step and I cocked the trigger, which meant he was about to be blown to kingdom come. Suddenly, he threw up his hands and cried, "Stop" and backed off and resumed policing the grounds. In the military, if you don't stop after three halts, you are dead.

To this day, I am forever thankful that this confrontation ended peaceably, and that I did not have to spend the rest of my life knowing that I killed a man.

The Reader

James Gorman

In 1948, I was born the only son to a college professor. My father, with four Masters degrees, was well respected and had reached the highest accolades of the academic world. He used to tell me to turn off the idiot box, referring to our ten inch black & white TV. He said, "Read a book, any book". "When you see a word you don't know look it up in the dictionary." "This is the only way you'll get ahead in life". This made no sense, turning off the idiot box and not watching Popeye, the Three Stooges, and Soupy Sales, too much of a sacrifice for a small boy. I felt he was taking his job too seriously by bringing it home with him. The consummate teacher and his rebellious student. I wondered if the father who is a plumber, tells his son, "Carry this plumbing wrench around, it may come in handy." Or if the carpenter says to his son, "Keep hammering that nail, someday you'll thank me".

In third grade, Catholic school, while fellow students were busy diagramming sentences, I was looking out the window daydreaming. It could have been a chirping bird or a squirrel scurrying across a telephone wire. I was lost in another world, until the sound of the nun's voice "Jimmy, Jimmy," broke my concentration. I could master the art of daydreaming better than anyone. Even being scolded with the cracking of a ruler on the back of my hand could not break my creative visualization.

In 1953, Ian Fleming, the author and creator of James Bond, the dashing British spy, was very popular. After my father finished the book, he would give it to me with a series of turned down pages. He wanted me to read the book without looking at the bent pages which he felt would rob my innocence and corrupt me. It was 1958. I was ten years old and curious. I read the bent pages only and told him I was ready for the next book. That summer I finished the entire twelve book series. The flow of words, thoughts and ideas became addictive. I had a hard time finding Bond girl, "Pussy Galore", in the dictionary. I did comprehend that she must have been very important; any reference to her resulted in a folded "do not read" page. In retrospect, my father in his wisdom probably knew that I would go right to the folded pages. This would suffice and he would not have to take part in that awkward father and son talk about the birds and bees.

My world was rapidly changing. I realized that reading could give me new material to get back to my favorite hobby of daydreaming. I turned off the idiot box and said good bye to Popeye although he was responsible for me consuming large quantities of spinach. I would rush off on my bike and spend countless hours at the local library. If it was in print, I wanted to read it; my father created a literary monster. Tom Sawyer taught me that if I looked like I was having fun washing my father's car, maybe my friends would help me and we could trade marbles and frogs. How exciting it was to jump on a raft with Huckleberry Finn and ride down the mighty Mississippi River. Hemingway and me running with the bulls at Pamplona. Catching the big marlin, down in the Florida Keys and drinking mojitas in the sunset. I biked with Homer in Saroyan's Human Comedy as we delivered war death telegrams in the Midwest. When I felt the pressure of life, I would run into the woods with Thoreau's Walden Pond. I desperately wanted to help Holden Caulfield protect all the Phoebes in the world. My sexual curiosity was soon satisfied by Henry Miller's "Tropic of Cancer" or Reage's "Story of O". Kerouac, Dickens, Orwell, Swift, Fitzgerald, Steinbeck and Melville—my head was going to explode! I memorized the vision of Joyce's "The Dead". The first time I can remember crying was seeing Fredrick March play Willy Lomax in Arthur Miller's "Death of a Salesman". I never realized the power of words and dialogue and the emotion they can evoke. I related to the character Hickey in O'Neil's "Iceman Cometh", as he walked into the bar of inebriated lost souls and whores and convinces them to cast away their delusions and embrace the hopelessness of their fate.

On a hot summer night I would run through the sprinkler, ripping off my wet tee shirt and yelling "Stella . . . Stella" at the top of my lungs, hoping I would turn the corner on to Tennessee Williams's French Quarter. Anything by O'Neil or Williams kept me spellbound. Perhaps I was not normal, so off I went into the literary world of self-help. I tried to see if there was a common thread between Dale Carnegie, Dwyer, Deepak Chopra and Joseph Campbell. Maybe it was time to sit on Freud's couch and be analyzed. Or look to the ancient sages of Socrates, Aristotle and Plato. So much to soak in—so little time.

When I was seventeen, the teacher and student finally bonded. We would retreat to our finished basement and drink fine scotch. He promised me he would listen and look at the lyrics to all my early Bob Dylan albums. In return I would listen to the entire recital of Dylan Thomas "Christmas in Wales". We were bonding with fine scotch and love for our Dylans.

There once was a best-selling cookbook entitled "You are what you eat". I think it was written by some anorexic vegetarian. Over the years, I have come to believe, "You are what you read". The choices you make are on the words you are exposed to; be it in any form of media, your choices in plays, movies and even music lyrics.

In the Bible, the literal "word" is referenced numerous times. My father passed away twenty years ago. When the moment moves me, I pour two shots of scotch. I take out a worn faded book with bent pages and with the words of Dylan Thomas playing in the background, I toast my hero, my father the professor. Class is out but the lesson continues.

I'm still daydreaming at the age of sixty three. When I grow up I want to be an author. You cannot stop aging, but no one can tell me to grow up. Someday I'll enter my name in the search box in amazon. com. Hit return key and get a hit.

Then I'll be a daydream believer.

Hats Off To Lilly, A Budding Writer!

Irene Maran

The children's room in the library stood vacant. Three rows of chairs were arranged in a semi-circle with one larger chair placed out in front. That would be my chair, the chair for the storyteller. Today I would be reading two of my stories to a gathering of children I had never seen before. It was my job to entertain them for an hour.

A group of chatty little youngsters entered the room and quickly settled down in their seats. I was happy to see almost every chair filled. This was an after school program which mothers and children could sign up to attend. There were a few brothers and sisters in the audience sprinkled with curious mothers who were still young at heart and eager to hear my stories.

Both stories were about Rocket, an orange box turtle and his true-to-life adventures. When I asked the audience if anyone had ever owned a box turtle, Lilly, a young girl, there with her older brother and mother, raised her hand. "I have a turtle," Lilly answered without hesitation, "His name is Henry!" Lilly's mother quickly pulled Lilly's hand down and said "No, she doesn't." Lilly was the youngest child present, but noticeably the most attentive and animated. One of my stories was entitled "Rocket Joins the School Band." When I asked if anyone played a musical instrument, Lilly's hand went up again as she blurted out that she played the clarinet with her two sisters. "No, she doesn't," her mother replied, "And, she has no sisters!" Some of the other children were anxious to reveal what instrument they played at home and in school, and even which musical instruments were used by other members of their family. Lilly shared the fact that she is on her brother's baseball team, since Rocket, my story book character, loves playing baseball. "No she doesn't," were three words her mother repeated many times that afternoon.

Among all the children in the library I found Lilly to shine brightly above the others. She had a vivid imagination and was always excited to express herself. "A budding writer and future author," I thought, and someone I would gladly encourage to attend my next reading group, in spite of all her spontaneous interruptions. She had all the prerequisites for a good writer. In Lilly's world, she owned a turtle named Henry, played the clarinet with her sisters and was a member of her brother's baseball team, "all fictional." I'd love to have Lilly join my writing group in another ten years, feeding me her creative ideas. Talent cannot be contained . . . not even by a mother's hand.

The Silent Bell

George H. Moffett

It bothered me whenever I passed by my church. This was not something new. It had been going on for many years. On Sundays when I attended church the feeling went way beyond being bothered. I felt a sense of deep frustration and loss. Our church bell was again silent. Why didn't the church bell ring and spread its melodic tones out over the community and remind the residents that the church was still reaching out to them?

In 1900 the bell found its first and only home in the steeple of the newly constructed First Methodist Episcopal Church of Bradley Beach. Each Sunday the bell was rung before the morning and evening services, plus on special occasions during the week. It was a glorious sound as it introduced the community to our new sanctuary.

My oldest and fondest memories of the bell "spreading the word" date back to the 1930's when I was a young boy attending Sunday school. John McLean, our Sunday school teacher, had quite a Scottish brogue which we tried to mimic without much success. He also had a sense of humor which held our attention while in class and kept us out of trouble, at least some of the time. That's about all I can recall concerning our class except for the fact that our sessions always ended five minutes early, much to the annoyance of the other kids in Sunday school. Mr. McLean would leave our Sunday school room and head over to the West Narthex of the church. We followed him as if he were the Pied Piper.

Upon his arrival there he would unhook the thick rope which reached up to the ceiling and disappeared through a hole to an unknown destination. Next, our teacher, who was small of stature and not very heavy, would muster up all the strength and energy he could to pull down on the rope. Lo and behold, after a couple of pulls on the rope, we heard a bell ringing—our bell. We took turns helping our diminutive leader ring the bell by grasping the rope when it was pulled down and hanging on it as it ascended back up taking us several feet off the floor.

Our teacher, probably not to his liking, but certainly to our delight, kept ringing the bell until each one of his faithful students made a couple of trips up towards heaven before he stopped. We always returned the following Sunday to partake of his class, but I'm not sure whether our motivation was to learn more about Jesus Christ or to ring the bell. I guess the reason wasn't important as long as we attended and received the Word of God.

During the 1950's a sound system designed by Mr. Blackwell, an electronic genius and a member of our church, was installed in the sanctuary. This system, which replaced the ringing of our faithful bell, made it possible for recorded music to be played over four speakers installed in the bell tower. Music was played twice a day Monday thru Saturday. On Sunday music was played before the morning and evening services to alert the parishioners that it was time to hear the Word of God once again. The system was used for many years until time took its toll, and, like many manmade systems do, it ceased to function.

For the next couple of decades the steeple remained silent as the decaying process got worse. As time went by, the steeple became the home for pigeons which necessitated closing up the sides of the open steeple for health reasons and to hopefully prevent further deterioration. At various times over the years discussions were held considering the ringing of the bell again, but nothing developed. The consensus of opinion was that the tower was unsafe due to deterioration. The fear was that pulling the rope and ringing the bell would create vibrations that could lead to the bell caving in the steeple.

The silence of the bell left a void in my life. I guess to me, the bell, my bell, became a symbol of the past. The bell kept prodding me to do something so it would not be silent any longer. It seemed to tell me, create more happy memories. Spread the bell's word to a new generation. Ring the bell!

After much thought I contacted a local engineer to see if he would be willing to volunteer his services to check out the stability of the bell and the steeple, to see if we could start ringing the bell again. He agreed. After a thorough inspection of the steeple and the apprehensive test ringing of the bell, all was declared safe and sound.

Without announcing my plans for the next Sunday, I went to the church earlier than usual to ring the bell at 9:30 a.m., a half hour before the church service started. Standing there in the West Narthex, with the rope in my hands, I felt my heart beating faster than normal. I placed my hands higher up on the rope, ready to pull down and ring the bell. After the second pull on the rope I heard our bell, my bell, once again send its message out over the community. I continued to ring the bell twelve times. I felt this would be an appropriate number as it took me back to the days of the twelve apostles as they served Christ.

After the morning service, seven year old T. J. Chamberlin asked me if he could help me ring the bell next Sunday. Suddenly I had flashbacks of myself seventy years ago ringing the bell. Time changes things over the years, but precious memories remain as powerful as the day they were created. Enthusiastically I responded "Yes" and told T. J. to be at the church next Sunday at 9:25 a.m. so we could ring the bell together.

Showing up on time, T. J. helped me pull down the rope and then hung on to it as it once again lifted another youth of our church several feet off the floor. T. J. was not the only person hanging on the rope that special Sunday. There was also a boy of seventy years ago hanging on right alongside of him.

The story of our bell didn't end there. The following Sunday, as I was getting ready to ring the bell, something totally unexpected happened. Mrs. Nicola Mulligan's Sunday school class appeared. The children came to help me ring the bell and ring it they did. I will never forget the wide eye stares and the smiles of excitement on their faces when they pulled on the rope and the bell rang. The awesome power of the bell has found a new life.

A Tribute to My Brother Nick

Elia R. Monticello-Reyes

For many years we celebrated Christmas Eve at my brother's house with the family. The house was always cheerfully decorated with holiday ornaments, delicious food, beverages, baked goods, many gifts and loving cheer. It was a gala event we looked forward to every year.

My brother Nick was a compassionate loving person and most of all, our family's hero. He stood by us unconditionally and was firm in his beliefs. His presence made us feel secure and safe and his handsome face was always a pleasure to look at.

Nick was a United States Marine and served in the Korean War. He was part of the division of Marines who were trapped at the Chosin Reservoir. He was most proud that they left no Marine behind.

After the war, Nick became an electrician with the Newark Housing Authority. He held that position for 34 years.

Nicholas J.A. Monticello died on July 25, 2005. He was named Nicholas after our father. The J. stood for Joseph, our mom's brother and the A. stood for Anthony, our maternal grandfather.

Six New Jersey State Police cars and two unmarked cars escorted the funeral entourage. My brother's son, Nicholas, is a New Jersey State Trooper. They led the procession and stopped at every intersection directing traffic.

At the entrance of the church stood an Honor Guard of New Jersey State Troopers and a bag piper who was playing the U.S. Marine Corp Hymn. As the family and friends entered the church the organist played "Amazing Grace."

The priest commented at the overwhelming display of love and devotion that was shown at the funeral for Nicholas J.A. Monticello.

At the burial site were two U.S. Marines. They folded the American flag and presented it to his wife, Pauline. They thanked her on behalf of the President of the United States and the U.S. Marine Corps for serving his country well.

My brother Nick will be missed by all of us. May his soul rest in peace.

Two Teachers

Alice Cooper Richardson

I took Spanish for two years at Oakwood Friends School. My teacher was a Jewish Spaniard who had been rescued from Europe after the Second World War by the American Friends Service Committee.

She never told me the story of why she needed to be rescued. I never asked.

If others knew, the story would have spread throughout the school. So I assume others did not ask either. All I knew was that she had no papers. No papers of birth, of parentage, of nationality. No papers of what we have all learned to call identity.

I will call her only Erica here to protect her identity, although in class I always called her "Miss Brown." She was about twenty seven years old. She was a good Spanish teacher. She insisted we learn both standard and Castilian, which required one to lisp somewhat.

I took my first class my junior year. My senior year Erica came to me and asked me to tutor her in American History, so she could become an American citizen.

Why me? There were all the faculty members who could teach her. There were other students far smarter than I. And yet she chose me.

My heart swelled with gratitude for the trust being given me. At night, Erica and I studied together. We read history. We discussed United States history. She read and I quizzed her. Our roles reversed from the classroom. Two young women together. Me, a lonely senior. Erica, a woman who had been through a war.

When she passed the citizenship test, Erica and I celebrated with cups of coffee and muffins I had baked in the dormitory kitchen. We laughed. We cried. We told tales of our work together.

It had been an incredible journey for both of us. I, uplifted by her faith in me. Erica—Oh! And Erica—because she was now a United States citizen and once again had an identity in the world.

The Person Who Most Influenced My Life

Kalinka Shumanov

I was born in Bulgaria, a small but very beautiful Balkan country called "The Land of Roses". Bulgaria is bounded in the north by Romania, on the east by the Black Sea, on the south by Greece and Turkey, and on the west by the former Yugoslavia. When one looks at the map of Europe, it's easy to see why this country had to suffer through the centuries. It was because of her location.

My grandmother and my parents were witnesses to horrible oppression and suffering. Bulgaria was occupied by the Turks for almost 500 years. After that came the Balkan War, WWI and WWII. "The Black Years" of Bulgarian history, as my people would call it, inspires many people to write beautiful stories, poetry and music of the past. My grandmother was a teacher and would tell my brother and me stories of brave men and women who were fighting the cruel and inhuman oppressors for the preservation of their language, religion and traditions. She would tuck me in bed and with her stories, place me in a world where miracles happened and good will always won. She was one of the most influential people in my young years. She was able to make me feel better when I was sick, lift my spirits when I was down, make me build my dreams for the future when the present was bleak. She was also very creative and made incredibly beautiful things for house decorating and our use. Most of these objects were sold during the German occupation for a little food.

So many things have happened since my grandmother died, but memories of her are always present in me. This is the connection with the past which gives strength to one's roots. The world of my grandparents and parents has changed. Some changes in technology and medicine have made life better, but the closeness of the family, the opportunity to have someone which links you to the past and "the way it was" is gone.

We have telephones to "keep in touch", psychologists to solve our problems and counselors to advise us about the future, but, we lost something very important, the closeness with the senior family members.

Tales From The Left Coast

Rebecca Wasson

I cannot count the number of times that I have occupied this very bench, enjoying the Southern California ocean, in the sunshine, waiting for the shuttle to LAX. I am accompanied by sea gulls happily flying overhead. There are little birds searching for something in the bushes. The bushes, which were ordinary yesterday, were transformed into the overwhelming scent of gardenia by a gentle warm rain. One cannot help but be enveloped by their magical, glorious, fragrant scent when standing near them. Plants and wildlife are all seemingly happy to be living in So. Cal.

The mountains offer their majestic beauty with an azure blue sky backdrop. The multi-million dollar mansions of Montecito and Santa Barbara are nestled there in all their glory. How could people living in those magnificent homes not be happy? I know for a fact and from personal experience that they are not happy, not all of the time anyway. We all suffer from the problems of life whether we are very rich or very poor. Happiness is temporary and fleeting and must be embraced when it is with us.

The Left Coast of California is home to the laid back, easy going, not to worry lifestyle. I can feel the tears welling up in my eyes. I don't want to return to New Jersey, I want to embrace the beauty of all that is here. I want to wrap my arms around it and keep it with me always. Of course, I cannot do this, it does not belong to me; it belongs to no one. It belongs to everyone.

I am very fortunate indeed to be away from the harsh, painful 2011 winter storms of New Jersey. Basking in the California sun is a joy but sometimes I feel that I am torn asunder in many directions. Torn between the people, places and things that are my life and my loves. So, until I visit next time, I say goodbye to paradise for now. I will see you in my dreams.

2010 Christmas Blizzard

Ruth J. Abramowitz

Years ago when I was a child we had blizzards that kept us indoors for weeks. My family had a farm in the Catskill Mountains and Dad ran a heavy rope line attached to a hook outside a window connecting it to the barn door. Holding on to that rope was the only way he could get to the barn and care for the live-stock. We had horses, cows and chickens. There was no indoor plumbing until I was three. Mom put little pails in one room of the house to be used for toilet duty. I recall her saying make sure you cover them before leaving. There were wood stoves in each room of the house with a pipe going up one wall to a chimney. We had a large fireplace in the living area that also heated the dining room. Our cellar was filled with canned foods, frozen meat, and Mom's baked bread, cakes, and rolls with honey. Bags of flour and sugar were always on the shelves. It was a different time and a simple life style. No cars to dig out of snow banks, no worry about getting to work by bus, train or plane. A path was cleared and we walked or hitched the horses to a wagon or carriage and with a shout of "ahoy" from Dad, off they would trot.

Saturday morning December 24th, 2010, I had planned to go shopping. The news report said 23 degrees. I thought, "I'm not going anywhere today", so I decided to spend my time writing and clearing files. The day passed with more cloudy skies and no sign of snow. Reports continued to warn everyone to stay indoors and prepare for the storm. Winds were starting to howl and I turned up the thermostat. I went to bed after eleven o'clock, checking to make sure my windows were tightly shut. Sunday morning I looked out to see my window covered with snowflakes. Over two inches of snow covered the cars in the parking lot. By noon people were told to call airports for flight closings, stay at home if possible and call emergency numbers for help. Those travelers, already on the roads, found themselves stranded, unable to escape the heavy winds or move their cars out of the drifting snow. We were in the midst of the worst blizzard ever recorded and it was Christmas time. People were told air travel was at a standstill. Hundreds of flights canceled and buses, trains, and cars unable to keep moving due to snow and windy conditions. It was a holiday nightmare. Announcements continued to tell everyone not to go out. Thousands of people far from home or leaving for family gatherings found themselves stranded at the airports. Hotel rooms were booked and those who could not get shelter had to remain at the airports or train stations, hoping for the storm to break so they could travel on. Mother Nature had taken over our lives.

Storms, fires, hurricanes, earthquakes and other natural disasters have been a part of our lives for centuries. A century ago there were less people, cars, buses, trains and planes. Fewer people drove cars. Transportation by buses, trains and planes had fewer passengers. We had open space, farms, parks, forests and homes with large acreage. Electricity was for lighting our homes and gas was used to run our cars. Oil and other fuels had not yet been taken from our land and oceans to satisfy our appetites for more and more power sources. As our way of life demanded more from Mother Nature's resources, we did little to protect the earth and sea from pollution and waste.

Are these natural disasters telling us something? Have we taken too much and given back too little to protect our environment? We can't foresee what will happen in the years to come. Our people will recover from the many disastrous events of 2010 and we will continue to use resources from the earth and sea. Nature will replenish its losses and the population will continue to use them.

The human spirit renews its powers every year. Let us make 2011 a better place by learning from the mistakes of the past. We can't control the weather. We can control our habits and behavior.

Third Grade Remembered

Gary S. Crawford

I remember that Mrs. Hamill, my third grade teacher, was very pretty. She looked a little like Liberace, like she could be his sister. When my Dad saw her at a school function, he remarked that she was "stacked". I guess I noticed that too, my young eight-year-old hormones getting a head start on things.

There were two classes of each grade. My best friend, Alex Moumousis, forever nicknamed Moose, was always in the other class. In third grade, we were together finally!

When Mrs. Hamill had to leave the room for any length of time, our Principal, Mr. Larson, came in to keep an eye on us. There were several best friend pairs in our class, Moose and I included, and we were all eight years old, and could not be left on our own for very long. The kids called Mr. Larson "Lead Bottom", behind his back of course, the name used by the sailors on the *McHale's Navy* TV show when they spoke about their commanding officer, Capt. Binghamton.

You had to be eight years old to be a Cub Scout, and the recruiting drive came to us. We attended a big meeting in the school's All Purpose Room, a gym and stage theatre all in one. Most of the boys signed up, and my Mom answered the call to be a Den Mother. As a Girl Scout, she had been involved in my grandfather's and my uncle's Boy Scout troops as a helper and knew what to expect from a bunch of boys.

My grandfather explained to me that the Scouts were a lot like all those lodges he belonged to. A bunch of people doing good things and learning about many things in the world, such as American Indian culture and the love of Nature.

As I was now a Cub Scout, Pop suggested that I write to the President, telling him all about myself and my family. A nice project; I went right to work on it. To President Kennedy, 1600 Pennsylvania Avenue, Washington DC. It was a few weeks later that I received a letter on White House stationery. It was a personal note from Evelyn

Lincoln, Kennedy's personal secretary, telling me that the President was busy but appreciated my letter, and asked her to write back and tell me how proud he was of me. I still have that letter.

Third grade was still a time of possible nuclear attack, so we had drills where we went to the hallway and crouched down against the walls, "duck and cover", shielding our heads from "the blast". There were still commies out there, and we were ready for them.

In my third grade year, my second grade teacher, Mrs. Hopkins, had a son who was a Navy jet pilot. Once in a while all the classes would go outside to the playground and watch him fly over several times. I really liked that and was proud, as my Dad was in the Navy Reserves at the time. Dad wasn't a flyer but worked the ground crew of the final days of the Navy blimps.

Mom painted a full 4 x 8 sheet of plywood into a huge skull for Halloween that year, which was stood up on the porch. Happy Halloween, it said, across the top and bottom of the skull. It was definitely a landmark, people actually drove by to see it. Maybe that's where my love of all things macabre started. Yeah, that's it, it's Mom's fault. On the back of the plywood was a huge Christmas card Mom also painted, wishing one and all a Merry Christmas from our family; the sign later displayed on the porch.

I'll never forget the day, November 22, 1963, when Mrs. Hamill was called to the office, and then walked back into our classroom and said, "I have some bad news. The President has been shot". We had a week off from school after that, and there was nothing to watch on TV but news coverage of the assassination. I was watching—live—when President Johnson was sworn in, Jackie Kennedy standing next to him, blood on her dress. I was watching—live—when Lee Harvey Oswald was walked through that police garage and Jack Ruby shot him. I was watching—live—the funeral procession—the horses and wagon hauling Kennedy's casket, Jackie and Bobby and Teddy walking behind. I was watching—live—the graveside services and the lighting of the eternal flame.

It bothered me to watch all of this, two weeks away from my ninth birthday, to see the man I wrote a letter to—the President of the United States—shot and killed and buried.

I remember my mother yelling about a coverup after the Warren Commission ruled on the lone assassin theory. I remember seeing the replays of the Zapruder film of the assassination seeming to get shorter and shorter, like things were being left out.

Thanksgiving was just a few days after the Kennedy disaster, and maybe because of that, I remember that this was the last year I had to sit at the kids' table.

My sister, almost five years younger than me, had the most gorgeous hair, these beautiful long golden baloney curls, extending past her shoulders. My Mom would fuss over her hair, which my sister couldn't stand, wriggling and fidgeting until Mom finally gave up and let her go. One day, while playing with the Strominger twins down the street, two years older than my sister, they grabbed scissors and gave her a haircut. Mom was devastated! She had to give my sister a short bobbed haircut to repair the damage, actually crying as she cut the rest of her curls off. Third grade boys didn't have problems like this.

This was the first year my grandparents took me along to Atlantic City for a convention of one of Pop's lodges. I spent a lot of time shopping and sightseeing with my grandmother while Pop went off to his meetings. We rode jitneys and we walked the boardwalk. We went in to see all the attractions, including the Steel Pier and the diving horse, Ripley's, and the wax museum. She didn't like to go into the Chamber of Horrors in the wax museum, so she went through the gate to wait for me to come out of the Chamber. As usual, I loved the creepy stuff and heard her calling for me. I hung out in there for almost an hour and she was tired of waiting. Another great attraction was the James Salt Water Taffy store, where ladies were wrapping candy on a conveyor belt right in the front window of the store. Seeing this, I couldn't help but think of the *I Love Lucy* episode where Lucy and Ethel were trying to keep up with the candy on the conveyor belt. I wish there was some way I could get in there and get that belt moving faster! Another favorite place was Taber's, a huge toy store on the boardwalk that could rival FAO Schwartz, at least to my young mind.

Dad traded in his cool 1956 orange-and-white Mercury for a new Ford Falcon early in 1964. The Merc was a cool car, lowered with fender skirts and noisy mufflers, but now Dad had a sensible family car that was good on gas. Not only that, it was the first new car that Dad ever owned. A milestone, I guess, but I missed that '56 Merc! So did Dad.

I attended my first funeral that year, some aunt of Dad's I didn't know. Mom and Dad figured that a third grade boy could handle this sort of thing. Looking spiffy in a suit and tie, they led me to the casket to pay my respects. Maybe some kids would freak out, but I didn't. Then off to meet all these relatives I didn't know, and assorted hugs and kisses from old ladies wearing too much perfume. We weren't there long, and Dad said his goodbyes and we went home. I think it took longer for us to get ready than the time we spent at the funeral home. I remember how the place was very cool, almost cold, lots of people wearing black, lots of whispering, and the smells of fresh flowers and too much perfume.

Another first that year was going on a boat into the ocean. Dad and I had fished and crabbed in the Shark River, but always from shore. We had a neighbor who owned a cabin cruiser and he invited us to go out one day. We didn't catch anything; it was more of a pleasure trip. Dad and I had a great time, but poor Mom, always prone to motion sickness, suffered greatly through the trip, losing most of that and the previous day's meals over the side.

Every class, from kindergarten to eighth grade, put on a play each year. In ours, I was to play the part of an old woman, dressed in a baggy dress, wig, and granny glasses. It was a fair part with quite a few lines, and Mom helped me rehearse at home. I had my part down and the night of the performance finally came. I don't know why, but I wasn't scared at all, while most of the other kids were dying from stage fright. We went on, the play went well, and we made it through. I got a few laughs for my old lady role, and of course, the proud parents in the audience gave us all a standing ovation. Later, when my Mom was talking to another parent, and being complimented on my acting ability, Mom told her that the part was perfect for me, as I was "born old." That was the first time I ever heard that expression about me, and certainly not the last.

There were no such things as school lunches back then. You lunch-boxed it or brown-bagged it or you went hungry. Milk was available, or you brought a thermos from home. We ate in the classroom, and if the weather was nice, chased out the door to the playground after lunch. If it wasn't nice out, we were stuck in our seats for our half hour of free time. We had hot dog day once a month. We would take a form home and our parents would order hot dogs for us. We took the form back in, with our money, and that Friday would be hot dog day. A nice change from PB&J.

We had parties in class all the time. Halloween, Thanksgiving, Christmas, Valentine's Day, St. Patrick's Day, Easter, and other occasions, usually featuring cupcakes from one of the class moms. We could wear costumes for the parties, just making sure they wouldn't be in the way during the class day. Moms often sent in cupcakes for a birthday boy or girl, and that day would become a party as well.

In the third grade, girls were still considered icky and infested with cooties, but many of the boys were secretly checking them out anyway. Cindy and Susan were very pretty, even at that young age. Kim was goofy and funny-looking, but resembled her older sister, Marcia, who was a sixth-grade knockout, and we hoped that Kim would catch up to her. Kathy with a K was silly and fun, and Cathy with a C was another one destined to become gorgeous. Leslie was cute and reminded me of Nancy from the comic strips. Rose was plain and dumpy and a very good friend. We play-acted scenes from the Patty Duke and Anne Bancroft movie *Helen Keller* on the playground together.

My buddy Alex the Moose laughed all the time, mostly when he wasn't supposed to. Glenn was my other buddy, the sarcastic one of the crew. Frank had a few screws loose, already insane at such a young age. Joe was round and cuddly, like a big teddy bear. Carl had red hair. The other Gary was the first one in our gang to have to wear glasses. Dave was always in trouble, in and out of school, and we were kind of afraid of him. Skipper was the class goofball, and his cousin Randy was the "new kid" that year, southern accent intact. Scott was also a goofball, playing second banana to Skip. Mark was really into sports, especially baseball, but Tommy was the athlete and we all knew he'd be a sports star someday. Tommy also had an incredible singing voice, especially in an Irish brogue, and he was always one of the stars in our class plays.

Lynette was in the eighth grade and was the office messenger. She would come in to our class twice a day—morning and afternoon—bringing papers to Mrs. Hamill. The room would go silent when Lynette knocked and walked in. It wasn't right for third grade boys to have to look at something like Lynette, who was far too mature physically for us to deal with. As my Dad had said, she was stacked. Long dark hair, hourglass figure, it just wasn't fair to have her in the same school. My buddy Glenn's sister, Claudia, also in the eighth grade, was equally disarming in appearance, but we weren't subjected to her twice a day in our own classroom.

We read *Highlights* and *The Weekly Reader* in class. At home, I received *Boys Life*, the Boy Scout magazine, in the mail each month. We had movies and film strips in class, always a welcome distraction. There would be an occasional assembly in the All Purpose Room, often with a guest speaker or entertainer. It was amazing how our teachers could herd so many unruly kids into and out of the rows of chairs on the gym floor without pandemonium erupting. There were always some kids who couldn't get with the program, but all in all, things went surprisingly well, considering how many kids were in motion at one time.

We lived a block from the railroad and on nice afternoons I would sit near the tracks and watch the trains go by. The engineers recognized me and waved and tooted their horns. Other times, some of us would play soccer in the neighbor's big yard across the street. We'd have bike races around the block. We'd go to the school and play baseball or basketball. Or just ride bikes to wherever we wound up.

If we were close to home, Mom would put out PB&J sandwiches on the backyard picnic table for us, with something to drink. On weekends, we'd be ordered out of the house in the morning and not expected back until five o'clock for supper. On weekdays, I'd have to do my homework before I could go out, which meant that sometimes I didn't get to go out before supper. House rules dictated that homework would not be put off until after supper. Period. Not negotiable.

Maybe I'm looking back through time through Norman Rockwell's glasses, but things were so much easier back then. It sure was nice to visit third grade again. I think I'll give Moose a call.

Two Poems

WHAT'S IT ALL ABOUT?

Milton Edelman

I'll tell you friend, when I was born
Just as naked as a fresh shucked corn
I did not try to hide my pride
Nor tell the world to look aside.

No shame or blame did I possess
In entry to this worldly mess
The only thought I did request
Was, Mother Dear, I need your breast.

With the greatest love of womankind
She nurtured me and cleaned behind
From endless hours she did not shirk
As I cried and cried and made her work.

Although her greatest love was shown
She was far from being all alone
The partner that she always had
Was none other than the greatest dad.

Since that day that was my birth
`I sojourned well upon this earth
And when I give my bones to park
My deeds alone will be my mark.

DEAR OLD "MISS MATCH"

Milton Edelman

The waters were calm and the day was bright
As we sailed on the bay with the greatest delight
Not a care was aboard, not even a doubt
As dear old "Miss Match" purred truly on route.

"Hi Skipper," "Hi Neighbor," and "Howdy My Friend"
To one and all a warm greeting we'd send
The air was refreshing, the beer helped somewhat
What a lovely way to get out of a rut.

The channel was deep as the buoys passed by
We could see as far as the sea touched the sky
When suddenly came a most peculiar sound
I yelled "Captain, Captain, we're hard aground."

Alas! T'was not the time to be merry
We spoke words not in the dictionary
We beckoned to all to see our demise
And soon came a craft of very small size.

He threw us a line, and quick as a wink
We were sailing on merrily, trying to think
Oh, what a wonderful world this place could be
If everybody could go out to sea.

The Famous Holiday Fire of 1997

James Gorman

(Dedicated to the brave volunteer firefighters)

Bob and Carol were ecstatic about spending their first Christmas at the old Victorian house in Cape May. They purchased the house the previous summer and used up all their vacation days to make cosmetic changes and minor repairs during the fall. It was the house of their dreams and Carol so desperately wanted everything to be perfect. Bob's parents would be spending the holidays with them, as there were many spare rooms in the house.

It was early Christmas Eve. A gentle light snow was starting to fall. Bob and his father began putting up the holiday decorations while Carol and her mother-in-law were caught up with last minute shopping. Bob used a paper torch to heat up the chimney flue to cause a draft which would help to get the fire started. Bob's father, Ted, was busy setting up the trains around the Christmas tree. Buttons, the family cat, seemed to be quite amused as she lay curled up on the reclining chair. Her tan coat and emerald green eyes were in sharp contrast to the yellow and black afghan draped over the back of the chair.

Since most of the chores were done, father and son decided to test out the rum-laced eggnog. Bob always knew his father had a drinking problem as Ted seemed to down one drink after another. But, this was to be the perfect Christmas, so Bob thought he'd be better off not saying anything. Bob stood back and looked around the living room, quite pleased with the way things were progressing. He wanted to make sure every detail was in its proper place so Carol and his mom would be surprised when they returned home. He lit the three candles that were in the bay window. The window with its wide ledge is where Buttons regularly curled up when no one was home. Then Buttons discovered the reclining chair. Bob remembered last winter when he and Carol had driven down to Cape May and noticed that there was a candle in every Victorian window. It's a tradition that works well with Victorian houses. Ted had gone into the kitchen mumbling. He had secretly put more rum into the eggnog. When Bob turned off the overhead light to get the full effect of the room, Buttons quickly darted from the chair and curled up on the braided rug in front of the fireplace.

The girls had just entered the house, laden with gifts. Everyone commented on how wonderful the decorations were and sat down for a toast. Ted said, "I know we said that we wouldn't exchange gifts till after Midnight Mass, but your mom and I have a special house gift that we'd like to give you now. It was too big to gift wrap so I have it in back of the truck wrapped in an old paint canvas."

Bob and Ted brought the heavy object into the house and laid it down in the center of the floor. Everyone was filled with excitement when the canvas was unraveled to reveal an old mahogany grandfather clock. Bob and Carol had always loved this clock. In fact, Carol had made many complimentary remarks when she first saw the clock in the house that Bob grew up in.

"This calls for another toast", shouted Ted, which would give him another opportunity to nip the booze.

Bob, who was very excited about the clock, decided he would set it up. Carol thought it would look perfect next to the fireplace mantle. While Bob was setting up the clock, the fire had lost its brilliance and started to smolder. Ted said he would attend to the fire and asked his son where the fire irons were. Bob responded that they were still packed in one of the many unlabeled boxes in the basement. Ted muttered under his breath and went off into the kitchen.

After taking another shot of rum, he rummaged through the cutlery drawer, finding an old ice pick. Its wooden handle and metal claws would be just what was needed to readjust the fire. Ted went over to the fireplace and gently pushed Buttons out of the way. He used the ice pick to rearrange the burnt wood and let some air under the flames. Soon the fire was roaring. He noticed Bob having a hard time setting the mechanisms of the clock. Getting up to help him, he put the ice pick on the edge of the mantle. As Ted set the clock as only he knew how, Carol said "Come on now, its 11:30 and we have to leave for Midnight Mass. You know it's going to be crowded and we decided it would be nice to walk the three blocks." "Mom, why don't you bring the afghan with you in case it's cold in church?"

"What afghan, dear?"

"The one that's on the reclining chair" she answered.

Quickly retrieving the afghan, they left the house, and then Bob realized he forgot his church donation envelope and ran back to retrieve it. He picked up the envelope and gazed once more into the living room. The ambiance and decorations could pass for a Norman Rockwell painting. There was a warm radiant fire coming from the fireplace. You could also see two bright green circles emitting from Buttons' eyes and the glow from the window candles bathed in orange and yellow light on the newly fallen snow.

Yeah, that was the last memory Bob had of his perfect dream house. There was a lot of commotion at church from the sound of fire trucks racing through the village. In fact, everyone left the church to see the famous fire of 1997, as it became known. Many people remember Carol uncontrollably crying as she moaned over and over, "How could this happen?"

But there was no answer on that cold Christmas Eve night because cats don't talk and the fire inspection was still pending.

But I have my own theory on how a Norman Rockwell living room became a house of black ash and horror. Don't quote me on this, like I said, it's just a theory. Well, here goes:

"At exactly midnight the grandfather clock struck out a loud gong. The vibration caused the ice pick which Ted had left haphazardly on the mantle to fall. The ice pick traveling in a southward direction, with its sharp edge exposed, ended up residing in the derriere of one Buttons the family cat. This sudden painful pricking of Buttons' skin caused him to seek refuge as fast as possible on that old secure bay window ledge. You see, Buttons never liked the plain old reclining chair. He enjoyed the reclining chair with the warm afghan. Buttons really didn't have time to think, he just wanted to get from point A to point B. When he hit the window ledge, he knocked the candle to its horizontal left side where the flame met the softness of Irish lace".

The charred remains of the house had been bulldozed and removed, leaving a vacant lot with a for sale sign.

Bob's wife, Carol, is in intense therapy—dealing with the trauma of the fire. She remains isolated, content to knit afghans for veterans.

Bob has become a dedicated volunteer fireman.

Ted has sworn off the drink and is involved with a twelve step program.

Buttons is seeing a cat therapist—trying to control his reaction to running in circles every time he hears a siren.

The Lunch Box List

Irene Maran

A bucket list consists of things you'd like to experience in your lifetime, but never have the time or opportunity to make them a reality. As we grow older it's that "do or die" attitude . . . do it now before you die! Sometimes the list we create for ourselves is a stretch or extremely unrealistic. Because of this, I never attempted to select anything "over-the-top." Since my expectations are not so grand, I have reduced my bucket list to a smaller scale referred to as "The Lunch Box List." My list is more attainable for me. I plan to start checking if off as soon as I can find a pencil and while my health enables me to complete it.

The first item on my list is "to go hiking." I don't plan to scale Mt. Everest as I realize at the age of 70, I could never make it to the top. Why would I think I could? I'll just settle for a good day's hike on the Appalachian Trail, with my backpack and guide, feeling great at successfully completing a three mile stint. While on the trail I'll close my eyes and picture myself climbing Mt. Everest. Knowing I'll never swim the English Channel, my next item of choice would be to take a winter plunge in the Atlantic Ocean with a local Polar Bear Club. I've often read about this yearly event in the newspaper. Seeing pictures of bathers charging in and out of the frigid waters and wrapping themselves in towels and blankets always gets me revved up. I'd love to be a participant and afterwards warm up with a steaming cup of hot chocolate and marshmallows. The icy water will either start my heart racing or stop it cold.

Each year I watch the New York City Marathon on television. My eyes tear up when the announcer highlights specific runners and the sacrifices they endure from start to finish. Most of them are running in memory of a loved one or have an individual goal to fulfill. The wheelchair participants and handicapped runners cause me to stand up and cheer for their dedication. As a senior, I don't think I can train for a long race, but I can certainly run a short 3K. I plan to find a charitable organization and sign myself up.

I'd love to go on a wild safari trip to Africa. My love of animals would make me the perfect candidate for this trip of a lifetime. I'd lodge at an animal preserve where I could observe some of the largest and most beautiful animals I've only seen up close and personal in zoos. Orphaned and endangered animals running free would complete the "Born Free" fantasy I've always dreamed about. A trip like this is very expensive so . . . in the meantime and while I save for it, I'll make my yearly trip to the Bronx Zoo and leisurely take pictures of all the wild animals who will pose for me. It will be a practice run for the real deal.

As strange as it sounds, I'd like to jump out of an airplane, much like our former President, George H. W. Bush did on his 70th birthday. I know I'd be clinging to my instructor all the way down, but only then would I gain the confidence to open my eyes and capture the magnificence of this overwhelming moment. I can feel the rush already. Geronimo!

I'm all set to take a short cruise with my children and grandchildren before senility and old age set in. It's something I attempted to plan before, but with work and school schedules, it was impossible. I'd like to initiate one big family trip where we can't hide from each other. The main purpose for this outing is for everyone to relax and enjoy each other's company, face to face, whether battling or having fun. In today's busy world we have less family time for socializing than ever before. I'm all for family bonding.

I believe my "Lunch Box List" is feasible and can be accomplished in a reasonable amount of time. If all goes well, I can always add more "food for thought" to my list and hopefully expand on it.

My Summer Book Reading Escapades

George H. Moffett

My fondest and happiest memories of reading books occurred during the summers of my teen years, but only on rainy days when the beach was off-limits. I would find myself stretched out on the porch glider in my brightly colored striped tee shirt and my favorite short shorts. Of course no shoes; it was summertime. I can remember the glider being located perpendicular to the front wall of my house so passersby would not distract me and take me out of my reading world. Reality would be a distraction. I would read after lunch when the churning of an empty stomach would not be a bother; when my daily chores were done, and when the prospect of several uninterrupted hours lay ahead of me.

It is intriguing to me that, over half a century later, I still have such vivid and detailed memories of my summer reading escapades. I can even remember convincing myself that I wasn't a slow reader. That I just took my time so no detail would escape me, especially when reading my favorite stories about the Civil War. I can remember getting so extremely tense during the horrific battles, hoping that the North would win, hoping that my favorite characters, both from the North and South, would not be killed. I felt so sorry for the wounded. I recall feeling their pain, their despair, and their loneliness through the visual pictures that passed across the screen of my mind. As I reminisce about my teen years I draw to mind that I could never understand how Americans could shoot fellow Americans. Now, in my senior years, the question I ask myself is how anybody can shoot someone else because of a difference of opinion. Why didn't the troops of the North and the South just reach a compromise? If only I could have taken some of those pages out of the book, rewrote them with a peaceful conclusion, and put them back in their place. I guess these feelings and questions that arise are indicative of what a good book is all about. Of how well the author took his innermost feelings and displayed them on the written page for all to experience.

After many years, probably decades, of not reading for pleasure, I am happy to report that I have taken all of my books out of their storage closets. They are now on the shelves of my newly constructed office at home waiting to be read. Just looking at the books stimulates and challenges my mind and begs me to pick one up and read it.

Reading books about war no longer grabs hold of me and piques my interest. Now my primary focus is centered on people and what makes them tick. What motivates them? What makes them so impersonal now? When I was growing up technology was not in the forefront; people were. Neighborhoods were a close knit group of families sitting on their front porches chatting with each other and their neighbors during the evening hours. The kids were out front playing games and horsing around with each other; not sitting alone as they do today spending hours mesmerized by texting and playing computer games. Now I don't read books for entertainment as much as I read them for growth; for understanding people. For finding ways to help other people mature. To show them they are victims of their own decisions and not the decisions of others. To guide them down the road of realization and comprehend that if they change their thoughts they will change their lives. What a challenge!

In these later years I will be saying so long to the many hours of watching television and saying hello to recapturing the summer joys of reading I experienced during my teen years. Maybe, as I stretch out on my couch and open up a book, I can once again visualize the scenes and be consumed with what I am reading. Maybe I can become a teenager one more time, at least for a little while.

My Girlfriend Corrine

Elia R. Monticello-Reyes

Corinne and I have known each other since the fourth grade in grammar school. We immediately became good friends because we had so much in common. In gym class we played volleyball. While on the swings in the playground, we would imagine all sorts of things we could do, like flying to a foreign country which we learned about in our geography class. We wondered about the resources and lifestyle of people in those far away countries.

We did everything together. We were chosen to be monitors in school and given the responsible of watching the students going up and down the stairway, reporting those who were uncooperative.

The school formed a weekly newsletter called "The Mercury." Corinne and I were picked to be reporters. Each week we would go into each classroom to observe their activities and events on which to report and publish in the newsletter. We enjoyed this very much.

Once a week we walked to the library to return our books and pick out new ones to read. We would walk down 14th Avenue holding hands. In the cold winter air we could smell the scent of cooking sweet potatoes. We stopped by the manmade wagon that held a fire under a grill cooking the sweet potatoes. They smelled so good. The vender informed us that the large sweet potatoes were three cents each. We purchased one, split it in half and shared the delicious sweet potato. It felt so warm in our cold hands.

After our visit to the library we walked home in a different direction so that we could see the variety of stores on Springfield Avenue. We loved to window shop for clothes, bridal gowns, furniture and accessories. It was great fun selecting what we liked.

After school we walked home together most of the way, carrying our books. When we reached the corner before parting to go in different directions, we would stop and talk some more. Graduation day was approaching and we knew we would soon be parting.

Here we are now in our "twilight years," still talking and giggling like when we were kids. Even though our health is not up to par, we continue to send each other greeting cards every year, talk on the phone, and always remember each other's birthday.

During our friendship in school, our parents and families also became friends. We both have so many wonderful fond memories to look back on.

Our Cat Pookie

Kalinka Shumanov

Our 17 year old cat Pookie deserves to be called a princess. She did not win a prize in some beauty contest, but she should have. She is really extremely smart, a natural acrobat and a perfectly self-groomed beauty. Pookie came from the animal shelter as a kitten some 17 years ago, black in color with a splash of white. When we visited the shelter, most of the cats were quiet or sad, not hoping to be free again. Looking at all those abandoned cats made me feel guilty not to be taking them all home. Suddenly, while I was reading the information on the cages, a little paw came through the bars of a cage and tried to touch my hand. That was it; the little orphan was trying to say, "Please save me". I instantly felt she was the one to take home. The workers at the shelter were kind and very happy to see the one "prisoner" leaving. While we were signing the adoption papers, they gave us instructions on how to care for the new addition to our family and recommended in very strong language to keep our new kitten in the house.

I had cats all my life, and never kept them indoors. We were lucky to own our home down at the Jersey Shore with a little yard in a friendly neighborhood. We brought our new pet home, wondering how she would adapt to our busy family life. We had seven grandchildren and a young Dalmatian puppy named Duke. The dog was calm and friendly and accepted the new kitten without reservations. They eventually became good friends and enjoyed each other's companionship. Duke even permitted the kitten to sleep in his bed and play with his toys. We tried for a while to keep the kitten in the house but it proved to be impossible. Finally, one day when letting the dog in the yard, Pookie ran out with him. We realized she was born to be free and let her enjoy a normal cat's life. She was clean and the most playful cat I had ever had. Pookie slept indoors but enjoyed her freedom. She climbed trees and jumped on low roofs watching the outside world. My husband and

I grew older and changed as normally predicted, but Pookie seemed to be frozen in time. She still climbs trees effortlessly, catches bugs and other invaders. She also grooms herself to perfection. There is a saying, "cats have nine lives", and I can see why.

Our Town

Rebecca Wasson

I caught myself complaining irately about the increase in property taxes and my inevitable summer parking ticket yesterday and then I came to a stark realization. Bradley Beach, New Jersey, is one of the greatest places to live. The town measures one square mile. It borders the towns of Ocean Grove and Avon-by-the-Sea. Included is an amazing segment of the Atlantic Ocean, sand and beach included. This gives many people, residents and tourists alike, great pleasure both during the daytime and the evenings. Summertime brings us a concert at the Fifth Avenue gazebo almost every evening, where all can be serenaded and sing along too. Our library has special events and is a place where most of us are on a first name basis. Many interesting conversations and tips on several subjects are discussed here. We have our own movie theater and our eateries have become special of late. Our fire department has informative open houses and is the host to the well-attended annual Art and Media event. The children stand patiently waiting on the sidewalk and love when the firemen drive down the street in their fire trucks on holidays and throw candy to them.

We have a Main Street, and yes, it is a typical Main Street USA. The financial woes of the country have not left us unscathed. We have also seen the typical budget cuts and administrative positions unfilled after someone retires. There are residents who have lost their homes to foreclosure; they have been kindly welcomed into our town, to get a new start. The mailman delivers unemployment checks to many residents. Summer Camp fees were raised by $50 per child and fewer field trips have been scheduled. This has not prevented the children from enjoying each other's company under the watchful and dedicated care of their counselors and administrators. Sometimes, the air conditioning in the Senior Center does not work. This does not prevent a large crowd from forming there anyway. Last week the meeting included pizza, beverages and a wonderfully frothy fruit cake with strawberries, bananas and whipped cream. The annual dues of $7.50 are still the best deal in town.

In summation, our town of Bradley beach is fortunate in many aspects. The ocean soothes our slumber; summertime evening air is filled with the sound of music. People come from miles away to partake in the treasures we possess. Best of all, my friends and relatives are here. I am a little closer to heaven in my dream cottage by the sea.

In Memoriam

Members of the Roundtable who are no longer with us, though their creativity and talent live on.

Lee Anderson	January 1, 1918-May 15, 2010
Ann Florio Marzano	May 11, 1926-July 16, 2010
Herbert Porter	June 15, 1934-October 7, 2008
Harriet May Savitz	May 19, 1933-July 20, 2008